# SKINNY MAN

# SKINNY MAN

## James Colbert

ATHENEUM • NEW YORK • 1991

Collier Macmillan Canada   Toronto

Maxwell Macmillan International
New York   Oxford   Singapore   Sydney

Atheneum
Macmillan Publishing Company
866 Third Avenue, New York, NY 10022

Collier Macmillan Canada, Inc.
1200 Eglinton Avenue East, Suite 200
Don Mills, Ontario M3C 3N1

Library of Congress Cataloging-in-Publication Data
Colbert, James.
    Skinny man/James Colbert.
      p   cm.
    ISBN 0-689-12098-2
    I. Title.
    PS3553.04385S5   1991
    813'.54—dc20              90-46731        CIP

10  9  8  7  6  5  4  3  2  1

Printed in the United States of America

For GLENN J. GRANNAN,
the original

# SKINNY MAN

# 1

Stan Lee said more to himself than to the girl, "My partner is never going to believe this." His crooked smile softened to a grin. He shook his head. "*I* hardly believe it. And I'm here."

The girl did not reply right away but slammed the shift lever from second gear to third. Then she groped behind her seat, brought out a camera, and said, "So take pictures."

So Stan Lee did. First he took three quick snaps of the girl: about five feet tall, maybe ninety-five pounds, and *round*, not one sharp edge on her. She sat on two telephone books just to be able to see over the wheel, her blonde hair blowing in the eighty-mile-per-hour breeze, blue eyes fixed straight ahead, breasts *right there*, perfect handfuls, nipples poking at her blouse's sheer material as the wind ruffled it.

*Goddam*, Stan Lee thought, smiling his slow smile again.

They were close now. Stan Lee smelled the water before he saw the white-on-green sign that read only CAUSEWAY. Just a few minutes before, they had left his cabinet shop in the warehouse district, an industrial area of two- and three-story warehouses adjacent both to New Orleans's downtown and to the Mississippi River. They had driven out the expressway, passing Charity Hospital, the Superdome, Central Lock-up, going over the six-lane, high-rise overpass, past the sprawling, above-ground cemeteries, quickly making their way toward Lake Pontchartrain and the Causeway. The Causeway was the longest open-water bridge in the world, two parallel spans straight as plumb lines and flat as low tables that ran across the middle of the huge lake, connecting New Orleans with the northeast corner of the state.

"It's twenty-five miles from toll booth to toll booth," the girl had said after she had described the kitchen island she wanted, and Stan Lee had said that, sure, he could make it. Then she had started bragging, telling him what *she* could do. "I've been across it in under ten minutes."

Stan Lee had thought about that for a moment, using his flat carpenter's pencil to scribble the numbers. By his figuring, 25 miles in ten minutes meant 150 miles per hour. Average.

"Under ten minutes, huh?" he had said in his dry, North Louisiana drawl. "Under ten minutes in an airplane, maybe."

"In a *rocket*," the girl had shot back, jerking her thumb over her shoulder, pointing at her low-slung red car, smiling but not taking her eyes off him.

Stan Lee had looked at the car, pretending to study it, knowing that she was up to something but not yet quite sure what it was; then he had ambled over to the car and popped the hood to inspect the big engine. It was nice all right, but hell, back home he had *built* engines better than that. He had looked back at the girl, giving her his slow, friendly grin, and said, "What is it, exactly, that you have in mind?"

"A bet," the girl had replied brightly.

Stan Lee had listened carefully as she had explained it the first time, then he had asked her to repeat it, just to be sure.

"It's pretty straightforward, I'd say," she had said, the least little trace of impatience in her tone. "I drive across the Causeway one way. You drive the other. We'll take my car, and we'll time it. If I'm faster, you build my kitchen island for free. If you're faster, you get me."

Stan Lee had taken his time with that one, looking from the motor to the girl then back to the motor. Sure, he had cut a few deals in the past few years—he had traded kitchen cabinets for various hand tools and portable equipment, for a new sink and commode, even to pay off his beer tab—but this kind of deal, this was a first. He had closed the hood firmly, making sure that it was down tight.

"My partner is never going to believe this," he had said for the first time, shaking his head. As an afterthought he had asked, "What's your name, anyway?"

"Karen," the girl had replied, and had gotten into her car, glancing quickly at her watch, satisfied but not surprised to see that she was a full five minutes ahead of the schedule that had been given her.

After Stan Lee had closed the big door to the shop and had gotten into her car, she had backed out of the short driveway, looking around as she had done so, trying to spot the man she knew was somewhere nearby—trying not to notice Stan Lee Carter staring down the front of her blouse.


"Why don't you just fucking wave?" Rick Trask said out loud. Slouched low in his seat, the powerful, German-made binoculars resting on top of the wheel, he could see Karen looking around, looking right and left, looking for him. Disgusted, he dropped the binoculars onto the seat and unwrapped a mint, annoyed by the noise the cellophane made, wondering why he had ever given up cigarettes. He put the mint in his mouth, put the car in gear, rolled slowly forward until he could turn into the narrow alley that ran beside the warehouse Karen and Stan Lee had just left.

*Stan Lee,* he thought, repeating the name to himself, saying it with a derisive whine. *What a fucking joke.*

The alley was so narrow the car door would only open partway. Rick glanced in the rearview mirror before he squeezed out, sidestepped to the front of the car, got up on the hood, able now to reach the only window on that side of the warehouse. He glanced back down the alley before he allowed the pry bar to slide out from his sleeve.

It didn't take much to force the window, one solid push down on the pry bar, and the lock snapped. Rick slid open the window, pulled himself up on the sill, scrambled in, standing very still just for a moment, in a crouch, feeling the low-level adrenaline buzz, the heightened perceptions, knowing he could back out even now and not lose a thing.

"Fuck that," he answered himself.

He was in the shop's small office. There were papers all over a cheap metal desk, yellow copies of invoices mostly, and an old mechanical adding machine. On the wall there was a picture of a big, chesty blonde with a calendar stapled beneath her. Someone had been throwing darts at the picture, aiming for the tits, Rick judged, by the look of it; the girl in the picture was smiling seductively, showing her perfect white teeth.

"That's the spirit," Rick said, and patted the picture as he passed it, going out into the shop.

He felt good now, into it, amused that Stan Lee had been so distracted he had left on the overhead lights. He went directly to the junction box and removed the faceplate, pausing only a moment to study the heavy-gauge wires that brought power into the shop; then he began to take rubber-handled tools from his pockets.

"Wire snips," he said, like a surgeon directing a nurse, boosting himself up with the wry sound of his voice. "Pliers." Sweat glistened on his forehead as he worked. His palms were damp.

He stepped away from the junction box, inspecting his work, and very nearly fell backward over a five-gallon bucket of glue.

"Shit," he said, before he saw what it was, then he dropped to one knee to examine the label. "No shit," he said when he saw the printed warnings. He took out a screwdriver to pry off the top, and even before it was all the way loose he smelled the clean, sharp, combustible vapor.

*My, my,* Rick thought, glancing back at the junction box, seeing the wires he had just rearranged. *It looks like we got us a fire.*


He had been glad to get out of there, that was for sure. By the time he had poured out all five gallons of the thick yellow glue, soaking it into the scrap bin and running it across the worn concrete floor, the fumes had gotten to him, making him dizzy and disoriented, hardly able to remember which lines he had crossed.

*Now there was a moment,* Rick thought, nervously laughing at himself, *flipping those switches.*

He felt fine now, a little sick to his stomach but fine otherwise, better by the second, in fact, almost giddy as he recalled flipping the switches, what had happened when he had hit the right ones: a giant electric hum had suddenly filled the whole first floor of the warehouse, vibrating ominously through it. Mixed with the smell of the fumes from the fast-drying glue, he had smelled rubber melting, beginning to burn on the wire, then the scorched-energy smell of ozone; and although he had taken off right then, running back the length of the shop, one shoe sticky with glue, nearly pulling off, he had hardly gotten back to the shop's office when he had felt the muffled thump of the vapor's ignition.

He had scrambled out the window, remembering to close it behind him, and gotten into his car. He had gone through the alley, coming out on the next street, and practically all he had to do now was to wait, wait about ninety seconds he figured, make the block real slowly while the fire smoldered, producing carbon monoxide, needing only more air to explode into flames. Then he'd nip off the lock and throw open the big garage-type door to the shop.

Rick edged his gaze around the corner before he made the turn, coming back onto the broad street that ran in front of the warehouse, past all the other old warehouses that looked just about the same—except that now he could see smoke seeping out of the warehouse the shop was in, wisps of it leaking out through the two front windows and, down at curb level, beneath the door.

Suddenly, he could feel his heart pounding.

He stopped in the driveway, right where Karen had parked just a few minutes before, and jumped out of the car with his bolt cutters, surprised to see that the door wasn't locked. Looking at the empty hasp, just for a moment it threw him; then he grabbed the door handle and yanked it, putting his whole shoulder and back into the effort, feeling as the door rolled up a big inrush of air, a back draft whooshing past him like some huge, angry intake of breath—and seeing inside the shop, not twenty feet away, a man standing near the top of the stairs, staring right at him, his eyes wide with surprise and with terror.

A fraction of a second later, the warehouse exploded.

Rick felt himself thrown back, slammed against the side of his car, away from the flames that immediately erupted. He threw up his arms to protect his face and stumbled back farther, moving away from the searing, ovenlike heat.

Inside the warehouse, bright yellow flames swirled up the columns and down the lengths of the beams. Blue-yellow flames leapt up where the glue had been spread. The man inside was engulfed by the flames, fire dancing over the length of him. He flailed furiously, waving his burning arms, thrashing at himself before he fell down the stairs and lay still.

"No!" Rick Trask bellowed. "No!"

# 2

Against the advice given him by the range instructor, his watch commander, and even the manual that had come with the revolver, Skinny had removed the side plate from his nickel-plated Model 19 Smith & Wesson. Undeterred by the complex of odd-looking parts inside, many of them connected by springs that ranged in size from small to tiny, he had disassembled it, laying the pieces out on his unmade bed. Kneeling beside the bed, leaning on his elbows, his long, skinny legs poking out of his wrinkled boxer shorts, during the two hours it had taken him to fit the pieces back together, by turns he had been bewildered, impatient, irritated, and finally angry: the revolver did not work any better than it had before he had fooled with it. The action was still stiffer than he thought it should be, and now, his reassembly complete, there was a grinding noise when he pulled the trigger, a grating catch as the hammer cocked double-action. No matter how many times he dry-fired it, clicking away as he walked around the apartment, aiming at the television set on the makeshift shelf, the flower patterns in the three-cushion sofa, the mounted duck in flight on the wall, when he held the silver .357 magnum beside his ear, he could still hear it, click-*grate*-click. Disgusted, he finally reloaded it and put it back in the holster, taking a few minutes to look out the window at the pool, looking for the girl who lately had been coming around in a white bikini in the early afternoons, oiling herself up for the sun as she squirmed around on one of the poolside lounge chairs.

Skinny was the resident policeman at the big apartment complex in New Orleans East, a job he valued not only because as a policeman he got to live there for free but also because it gave him a line on all the other residents, including the girl at the pool, who he was about to have the time to check out pretty thoroughly—Skinny was only on the second day of his thirty-day suspension from the New Orleans Police Department.

"Fuck," he said out loud when he saw that the girl wasn't there. "Fuck," he said again when he looked back at the revolver on the bed.

He picked up the revolver, unloaded it, and began to dry-fire it again, holding it inverted beside his ear, listening for the grate. Disgusted again, he started to reload it but stopped when the girl suddenly appeared, coming into the pool area from a new direction, wearing a bathing suit even more revealing than the one she had worn the day before.

"Holy fuck," Skinny said reverently when she adjusted the top to the suit.

The phone began to ring.

He ignored the phone, and without looking at it, flicked the revolver closed, not wanting to miss a thing; and he was standing just like that—at the window, steadfastly refusing to acknowledge the phone, the revolver in his right hand, clicking away—when the +P+ cartridge he had just put in the cylinder rotated in front of the hammer.

In the small bedroom, the sound of the shot was a concussing, ringing force.

Startled, Skinny jumped back and bumped against the wall, momentarily uncertain just what had happened but figuring it out quickly enough. He held up the long silver revolver and looked at it admiringly.

"Skinny'll say this," Skinny said out loud, referring to himself as he always did, as if to another person, "this son of a bitch *does* work."

His ears rang fiercely, but behind that ringing he heard the persistent ringing of the phone.

"What?" he answered it, speaking even more loudly than he usually did, almost yelling into the receiver, his voice harsh and nasal.

He heard sounds, but they were indistinct and muffled. He put his little finger in his other ear, worked it around vigorously, shifted the phone to that ear.

"What?" he said again.

"You gone deaf?" the small voice asked. "This is Theriot. Theriot. You got it this time?"

"Yeah, Skinny's got it," Skinny said.

Theriot was one of the detectives in the bureau. Normally a quiet man, with a couple of beers in him he became nearly as loud as Skinny was without the beers.

"So, Skinny man, how's the vacation?" Theriot asked, and chuckled.

Skinny did not bother to reply to that. He knew his suspension was regarded with varying degrees of amusement throughout the bureau, but faced with the prospect of a month without pay, it did not seem particularly funny to him. The problem was, Skinny drove like he did just about everything else, brashly, unpredictably, and without much regard for consequence. And while those same traits made him extraordinarily successful when he worked undercover, as a driver he was a one-man disaster. No matter how old or beaten up a car when it was assigned him, within a month or two it looked considerably worse: in the previous twelve months, he had totaled four different unmarked police cars. After the third, he had been given a warning; after the fourth, a thirty-day suspension.

"So, anyway," Theriot went on, "I'm on Julia Street, in the warehouse district. A warehouse burned down. They just got the fire out—"

"Yeah?" Skinny interrupted him. "Now you working for the fire department?"

"Hey, give it a rest, all right?" Theriot replied to the slur. "*I* didn't get you suspended."

Skinny rolled his head back and rubbed the tip of his unshaven chin.

"Yeah, so?" he conceded.

"So, we got a crispy critter here. One of the owners, a guy named Mitchell. The place burned for quite a while, and it looks like he was inside it the whole time. The preliminary report is arson—which makes it murder."

"Skinny knows what that makes it," Skinny said sourly, and just then, he saw it, the waist-high bullet hole in the wall. Alarmed, he quickly stepped over to it and bent at the waist to put his face close to it. He was more than a little relieved to see that the bullet had struck a stud and stopped right there, two inches into the wood.

"The other owner is a guy named Carter," Theriot went on as Skinny continued to examine the hole, curiously poking a finger into it. "Stan Lee Carter. He's here, too, and I been talking to him—wait 'til you hear *his* story."

In the splintered wood, Skinny could see the glint of the bullet's copper jacket. He knew he couldn't just leave it showing like that, so pulling out the long, knotted cord on the phone, he went into the bathroom to see what he could find to fill the hole, not really listening as Theriot recounted the story Stan Lee had told him, something about a race across the Causeway. He picked up his family-size tube of toothpaste and went back into the bedroom.

"The reason I'm calling you," Theriot finally concluded, "is that the girl lives in your apartment complex."

"Yeah?" Skinny said, using his thumbnail to peel off the thick, membranous crust that had formed in place of the cap.

"Yeah. My boy here got a look at the parking sticker on her car. He noticed it because the sticker is green and the girl's car is red, even the bumper."

Skinny squeezed toothpaste into the hole in the wall.

"What's she look like?" he asked as he filled the hole to overflowing.

"She's blonde," Theriot replied. "Blonde and short, maybe five feet tall. Blue eyes. And built. Round, he says."

Skinny whipped his head around on his cranelike neck, looking at the girl on the lounge chair, all greased up now, leaning back.

"You know her?" Theriot asked.

Skinny's eyes were bright green in the sunlight that reflected from the pool, bright green flecked with yellow. He licked his lips.

"Not yet," he said.

# 3

The way Skinny figured it, it wasn't like he had a whole lot else planned. He was supposed to take his father fishing sometime, but he had managed to avoid that long enough that another few days wouldn't matter. And he had planned to go out to the police firing range—which was why he had been fooling with his silver gun in the first place— but since he was on suspension, he wasn't even sure whether or not they would let him shoot. So he could either sit around and watch the toothpaste ooze out of the hole he had shot in the wall, or he could go on down to Julia Street to see what he could find out about the girl. It wasn't what Skinny called a real difficult decision.

He dressed as he usually did—in faded jeans and a sleeveless green fatigue jacket—and he touched up the hole in the wall, sprinkling some baking soda over it, improving the color, before he went outside.

On the way out of the parking lot, he looked around briefly for the car Theriot had described, but he hadn't really been listening, and two or three different cars seemed to fit the bill. He saw an opening in the traffic on the street and jumped into it, his pickup truck bouncing over the curb, shrugging to himself when he glanced up in the rearview mirror and saw that the exit from the lot was a good fifty feet away from the place where he had actually left it.

Coming in from New Orleans East, the six-lane expressway was elevated all the way to downtown. One arm out the window, cruising along about fifty feet in the air, well up over the safety rail in the cab of his truck, Skinny looked out at the view. It was flat all the way to the river, flat and green, the treetops interspersed with rooftops, church spires, and worn-out industrial works. Off in the distance, he caught a glimpse of the ball field where he had played ball as a kid. He turned off toward the river, looping around downtown, and worked his way into the warehouse district.

It wasn't hard to find Julia Street, it was the one with all the activity. Two fire trucks were parked in the middle of the street, the firemen collecting hoses and various equipment. A marked police car was parked nearby, a uniformed policeman inside it, filling out a report. A van from the coroner's office was just leaving. Skinny stopped right in front of the big door to the warehouse, pulling into the space the coroner's van had just left.

The old warehouse had been gutted by the fire. What remained was a shell. Sunshine streamed down through the burned-out roof and second-story floor. The big woodworking tools were warped and blackened hulks, covered by charred debris. The smell of water-soaked cinders was nauseatingly pungent, and pervasive.

Detective Mike Theriot was talking with an evidence technician, telling him the photographs of the scene he wanted, when he saw Skinny come in through the big door, his arms flapping loosely at his sides, his long legs kicking out, overextended, as if he were stepping over furrows in a freshly plowed field.

"Fuck me," Theriot said to himself. "Give me a minute," he said to the technician.

The technician looked around, saw Skinny, and waved.

"Hey, Skinny man," he called out. "What are you doing here? I thought you were on suspension."

"What's suspension?" Skinny replied, smiling brightly as he stepped over the rubble.

Theriot gave the technician a hard look.

"You want more to do?" he asked.

The technician moved away a few steps, then turned back and aimed his camera at Theriot, snapping a picture as Skinny came up beside him.

"You got Skinny's bad side," Skinny complained.

"I got what I *needed*," the technician laughed.

Theriot did not share their good humor.

"I told you *not* to come here," he whispered furiously to Skinny, ignoring the picture. "If the captain sees you, it's my butt."

Mike Theriot had been in the bureau less than a year. His straight black hair was parted on the side, long in front, and fell across one side of his forehead at an angle. He tended to wear dark, off-color suits—maroon, chocolate brown, army-blanket green—and wide, one-color ties that matched the suits exactly. He almost always carried a cheap chrome flashlight that was over two feet long. Skinny thought he was nervous.

"Chill out," Skinny said. "Skinny knows what he's doing."

"That I kind of fucking doubt," Theriot said sourly.

"Your ass hurts," Skinny replied in a friendly way, looking around, surveying the scene. "This place is a mess."

"That's years of experience speaking, right?"

Skinny did not dignify that with a reply.

"You solid about the arson?" he asked, suddenly serious.

Theriot seemed to think that over for a moment, then shrugged.

"Very solid," he said. "The wires in the junction box have been tampered with. There's an empty five-gallon bucket of glue that the owner says was full—"

"Glue?" Skinny said.

"Glue," Theriot repeated. "Fast-drying and very combustible. They use it to stick down plastic laminates—countertops, stuff like that. Whoever did it shorted the wires, poured out the glue, turned on the juice. The wires got hot and sparked the vapor."

Skinny looked around until he spotted the charred junction box, seeing even across the warehouse the wires that were hanging out of it.

"What about the guy who was fried?"

"One of the owners," Theriot replied. He tapped his long flashlight against the side of his leg. "He could've done it, but if he did, he worked awful hard to get himself killed in the process."

Skinny looked back at Theriot, waiting for him to explain what he meant.

Theriot eyed the evidence technician before he went on.

"The assistant chief said the arsonist knew a lot about fires." He tucked his long flashlight under his arm, then brought up his clipboard so he could read from his notes. "When the glue vapor ignited, there was a flash fire. That fire burned up the oxygen and began to smolder, producing carbon monoxide—which is combustible." Theriot looked from his notes to Skinny, his brow furrowed earnestly. "I never knew that. You see a house filled with smoke, the *smoke* is explosive. The whole house is like a big bomb—that's why you see firemen cut holes in the roof, to vent that shit out of there before they open a door."

"What happens if they open the door first?"

"They get knocked on their ass is what." Theriot glanced again at his notes. "As soon as the fire gets more oxygen, the carbon dioxide explodes. The chief said he knows that's what happened here because the place went up so fast."

Skinny thought about that for a moment.

"So how did the arsonist get back outside after he'd sparked the vapor?"

Theriot waved his clipboard at the far end of the warehouse.

"Through the office. He closed the door and went out the window. All he had to do then was to open the front door, and boom, good as dynamite." Theriot jerked his chin to indicate the big door Skinny had come in through. "And the explosion blew *out*. So if the crispy critter did it, he had to have charged back inside, into the fire, to get himself cooked."

"You checked the window?"

Theriot nodded.

"The lock is broken, but it may have been like that already." He waved his clipboard again, this time indicating the man standing beside what had been the office. "He can't remember whether or not it was broken before."

"That's the owner?"

"Yeah," Theriot said, and rubbed his chin with the back of his wrist, sneaking a glance at the man before he looked back at Skinny. "What a piece of work he is."

"Yeah?" Skinny said. He ran his hand through his hair front to back, then put that hand in the side pocket of his jacket. With his other hand, he unzipped the jacket a few inches and absently scratched the hair on his chest. The way it was looking to him, none of this was his problem. It did look like it could be fun, but he wasn't going to get a piece of it. He was on suspension. And if the girl *was* involved— even if she had just lured the piece-of-work owner out of the building—chances were she was already good as gone, anyway. It was getting on time to pack it up before the captain passed by and saw him playing policeman.

"Yeah," Theriot went on. "The guy thinks he's back in the Old West or something. He said he's from up around Bossier City—maybe that explains it."

Skinny zipped up his jacket, getting ready to leave.

"Explains what?" he asked.

"He said he's going to put a price on the man's head who set the fire," Theriot chuckled. "I asked him if he was going to circulate posters. Maybe get up a posse."

Skinny looked at the owner again. He was a cracker, all right. Skinny could see that in the oversize knuckles in his hard, bony hands and in his prominent Adam's apple, big as a golf ball up high in his throat. He was wearing brand-new blue jeans without a belt and a knit yellow sports shirt with a ribbed white undershirt beneath. His hair glistened with hair tonic, and he had the first real below-the-ear sideburns Skinny had seen in years.

"What's his name again?" Skinny asked.

"Stan Lee," Theriot replied. "Stan Lee Carter. Three words. Can you believe it?"

"Hey, Stan Lee," Skinny called out.

Stan Lee looked their way almost eagerly, ducking his head as he smiled cordially, showing just the tips of the perfect white caps on his teeth.

"How much of a reward are you going to offer?"

Stan Lee's smile faded and was slowly replaced by a determined expression.

"I aim to put ten percent of my insurance toward it," he replied in a slow drawl.

"How much does that come out to?"

"Forty thousand dollars," Stan Lee said. "I figure that ought to scent up the hounds."

Theriot and Skinny exchanged glances, then they both stared at Stan Lee.

"Skinny'll talk to the man," Skinny volunteered after a moment. He flapped his arms as he started toward the rear of the warehouse, Mike Theriot just two steps behind him.

# 4

*Look at them come*, Stan Lee Carter thought, vaguely amused, thinking of the two Catahoula hounds his daddy had kept on the farm. They had that same look about them, bright-eyed and eager, like when he had taken the scrap bucket outside after dinner. The one in front, he was a study, wearing rags that should have been put out on a scarecrow. The other one was shorter and heftier, dark complected, dressed up fancy but with something of a beagle-dog look about him. Those big brown eyes, maybe.

Stan Lee brushed his yellow-calloused palms one past the other and pretended to inspect his big hands as he did so. He did not want to look at those two with too much interest because he knew from his own experience that you did not watch the police too closely. You looked away from them, pretended to be afraid and caught a glance or two out of the corner of your eye. Otherwise, it made them wonder what you were up to—which was just what he didn't need.

*Mitchell would've, though*, Stan Lee thought, still looking at his hands but thinking of his partner. *Mitchell would've stood there staring until they'd have thought he was sick in the head.*

Stan Lee had tried to explain it to him, but it never had seemed quite to take: it wasn't the policeman's fault when you got put in jail, not when you were guilty. And they sure as hell had been guilty, caught right in the middle of a job.

Stan Lee had done the driving, waiting outside in his old yellow Cadillac, and Mitchell had actually gone in, pulling a few things off the shelf before he went up to the counter. Usually, he had gotten himself some kind of snack, some Spam and crackers, maybe, or cinnamon rolls; and if they needed it, a quart of oil for the car. Then Stan Lee had watched through the window as he went up to pay for it, waiting until his groceries were bagged before he took out his gun. Surprise. That was the part Stan Lee had liked best, seeing the clerks' faces when they saw that big gun, the way it got their attention. One second they'd just be going through the motions, making change or whatever, and the next, there they were, in the middle of something they sure as hell would remember. He and Mitchell had pulled it off twenty-three times, too, before, on the twenty-fourth try, a policeman had pulled in right beside him in the convenience store lot to get a free cup of coffee.

"Look at it this way," Stan Lee had offered. "If it had been one of them tests back in school, missing one out of twenty-four still would of got you a A."

But Mitchell never had come around on that one, even though they'd had five years up at Angola to get over it and fifteen years since then when things had gone a whole heck of a lot better. Ever since they had discovered insurance.

Way out back on his daddy's property, down a dirt road that almost wasn't there anymore, years before, his daddy had parked an old silver Airstream trailer. After they had pulled off a job, and later, after they had gotten out of Angola, Mitchell and Stan Lee had stocked up on beer and had gone out to the trailer to drink it. Sometimes they had stayed out there for days, drinking beer, sleeping, then drinking some more. The old trailer was a mess and didn't do much more than keep out the rain—it didn't even do that real well after Mitchell had shot up the roof—so when Stan Lee fell asleep with a lit cigarette and accidentally set it on fire, they hadn't considered it much of a loss. Stan Lee had told his daddy about it in passing and hadn't thought much more of it until a couple of weeks later he had happened to be there when the insurance agent had come by with a check for six thousand dollars—which was just a bit more than twenty-three armed robberies had netted Mitchell and him, not including the snacks and the oil.

Stan Lee remembered that check as a turning point in his life.

"Never let your insurance lapse," his daddy had advised him, proudly displaying the check, and once Stan Lee had gotten some, he had never been without it again.

Mitchell, Stan Lee recalled, had been a slow starter until he had seen how much money they could make. Stan Lee had insured his old Cadillac, and Mitchell had gotten a job at a gas station, towing in cars. They had driven all over the parish until they had found an intersection they both thought looked pretty likely, then they had waited until Mitchell had gotten a call for the wrecker that would take him right near there. The way it had been supposed to work, Stan Lee was supposed to roll through the stop sign and hit Mitchell in the side as he came down the highway; but while Mitchell had done his part just fine, coming along nice and steady, the first couple of tries Stan Lee had seen that big tow-truck bumper coming and had stopped at the last possible second.

"Goddammit, Stan Lee," Mitchell had complained after he had backed up from the third run. "What is the matter?"

"It's not the easiest thing I ever did," Stan Lee had replied, ducking out of the motorcycle helmet Mitchell had thoughtfully provided, "ramming into the side of a truck."

Mitchell had taken the helmet out of Stan Lee's hands and had mashed it down on his head, backward, so that Stan Lee couldn't hardly see a thing.

"I'll blow my horn when it's time," Mitchell had said. "All you do is mash on the gas."

Sitting there with that old helmet on backward, Stan Lee had felt like a bit of a fool, but when he had heard the horn, he had done his duty and stepped on the gas, lurching into a collision that had damned near killed him.

"Man, if accidents make money," Mitchell had said right after the wreck, removing Stan Lee's helmet before the police got there, "we're rich as creases."

"Hot damn," Stan Lee had muttered around his broken-off front teeth. "It looks like we found us a profession."

"We better get you a mouthpiece for next time," Mitchell observed, "to go with your helmet."

What Stan Lee remembered most from the following few weeks was the taste of baby food washed down with Budweiser beer—and, of course, the first of the checks.

*We had us a time*, Stan Lee thought fondly, beginning to realize how much he would miss Mitchell.

"What I aim to do," he said to the two policemen when they got near, "is to find the man set this fire and nail him to a post by his pecker." He took one last look at his hands. "Then I'll start my own fire, the kind we use back home to roast up a beef."

He glanced at the policemen real quick, out of the corner of his eye, and saw Theriot grinning.

*They like that*, Stan Lee thought, grinning himself, playing it real dumb. *They think it's some kind of a joke.*

\*          \*          \*

Skinny believed him. He heard that flat, slow twang, and he saw Stan Lee's pale, almost colorless eyes, and he believed him in a second. There was real country in there, not cowboy-boot country but mean, shoeless country, and with it the kind of matter-of-fact violence that made Skinny's blood run cold, like wringing a chicken's neck just to have dinner or cutting the legs off a frog.

He said, "You could invite the neighbors in for the barbecue—get some potato salad and make a day of it."

Stan Lee turned to face him but would not look right at him, seeming to focus instead on his shoulder.

"Could do that," he agreed.

"Jesus," Skinny said, and ran his hand through his hair, front to back.

"So, anyway," Theriot began, heading off trouble, "this girl walked in, offered to race you in her car, and when you got back, the building was on fire."

Stan Lee reached into his shirt pocket, took out a pack of unfiltered cigarettes, shook one loose.

"There's a little more to it," he said, and pulled the cigarette from the pack with his teeth, "but I guess that's roughly it." He took a big, worn Zippo lighter from the front pocket of his jeans, opened it using both hands, lit his cigarette. "She just wanted to get me out of here," he went on, narrowing his eyes against the smoke, "so her friends could get in and set the fire."

"Why didn't they just come in when you weren't here?" Theriot asked.

"Couldn't," Stan Lee replied. He took the cigarette from his mouth and held it between the very tips of two of his fingers. "Me or Mitchell—Mitchell, that was my partner—

one or the other of us was most always here. I lived upstairs, had a bunk in the back."

"Where did Mitchell live?"

Stan Lee smiled thinly as he inhaled more smoke, then blew it back out of his nose.

"He kept a room up over the Hummingbird Grill. He was kinda partial to the ladies."

Stan Lee's thin smile made Skinny think of a boy in a high school locker room, caught looking at centerfold pictures.

"Mitchell came in early this morning," Stan Lee went on, his smile fading. "He did that sometimes, came over here to sleep when he'd been out late—he knew the tools would wake him when it was time to get up." Stan Lee pinched a flake of tobacco off his tongue. "Maybe he caught 'em setting the fire, or maybe he just got caught in it after it started. Don't matter much, the way I figure it."

"Too bad for your friend either way, right?" Skinny observed.

Just for a moment, Stan Lee's pale eyes fixed on his eyes. Skinny held the gaze, but it took an effort. Stan Lee bothered him considerably. His eyes were too clear, as if there were nothing behind them, and hard as glass.

"That's right," Stan Lee said softly.

"So, Stan Lee," Skinny kept on, brushing at his hair as if he'd felt something in it, "the big question is, why would anyone other than you want to burn down your building?"

Stan Lee did not reply to that right away but bent one of his big ears double and scratched at the back of it.

"We've had a couple of offers to buy the building," he said finally, and let go of his ear. "If I were you, that's where I'd start."

"Who made the offers?"

"A lawyer's been coming around, being real pushy. Said he wants to build condominiums."

"Do you remember the lawyer's name?" Theriot asked, clipboard and pen at-the-ready.

"Mitchell's got his card, up in his room."

Theriot considered that for a moment as Stan Lee took a final pull on his cigarette, then put it out by pinching off the ash.

"That doesn't quite figure, Stan Lee," Theriot concluded. "If a guy's going to burn down your building, he's not going to give you his card before he does it."

"Could," Stan Lee replied. Before he went on, he rolled the cigarette butt into a ball and put it into his pocket—an unconscious habit Skinny noted with interest. There were only two places he knew of where men were required to pick up their own butts, in prison and in the service, and Stan Lee didn't look like he'd spent a whole lot of time in the service.

"But it wouldn't make much sense—" Theriot began.

"Unless the building owner's done time, right, Stan Lee?" Skinny interrupted, taking his guess. "Then he might risk it. He might try to make it look like the ex-con owner was working a double play, burning down the building for the insurance before he goes on to sell it—it even sounds like something a lawyer might come up with."

Stan Lee smiled hopefully.

"That's sort of the way I figured it, too," he agreed.

"That's why you're offering a percentage of the insurance as a reward, right?" Skinny went on in a friendly way. "It adds an incentive for whoever's looking into it to nail someone else—the insurance company isn't about to settle up if *you* get charged with the arson."

Stan Lee shifted his stance slightly, for the first time conveying unease.

"I wasn't here," he protested, his accent deepening. "I told you that. The girl come and got me."

"So Stan Lee's asking us to make a pretty basic assumption," Skinny continued, acting like he had shifted his attention to Theriot but keeping his shrewd eyes locked on Stan Lee. "He's asking us to assume that he didn't do it." He cocked his head to one side. "Or maybe he's just offering to buy a case against somebody else."

"I ain't offering to buy nothing," Stan Lee snapped in a flat twang. "Don't have to. I'm not the one did it."

"Skinny's just thinking out loud," Skinny said agreeably. He raised and dropped both his shoulders at once, then looked over and winked at Mike Theriot. "So let's talk about the girl—"

"The way I see it," Stan Lee cut him off pointedly, his voice flat and hard, "when a man's partner is killed, he's supposed to do something about it. If he's just a friend, you got a choice. But a partner, that's a different matter—it looks bad if you just let it go."

"It's bad for business, right?" Skinny interjected.

"You bet it's bad for business," Stan Lee replied hotly, glancing at Skinny before he glanced away, obviously uncertain how to read him. "I want the man caught set this fire, so what I'll do"—he looked right at Skinny—"I'll post my reward in cash."

"Hot damn," Skinny said quickly, smiling brightly, unknowingly saying the same two words Stan Lee had said after his first arranged crash.

# 5

Skinny had been called Skinny since he had been thirteen years old, when that particular physical attribute had become even more readily manifest. Already thin, one summer he had grown over three inches, but he had added very little weight to that new height. At six feet two inches tall and one hundred twenty-five pounds, thin no longer quite applied to him, he was *skinny,* a condition that had caused him no small amount of grief.

Skinny had been born and raised in Gentilly, a racially mixed neighborhood not far from the apartment complex where he currently lived, at a time when the changing body of federal law had brought about substantial damage to his own gawky body: newly militant black youths repeatedly singled out the skinny white kid who lived in the shotgun-style house on the street near the ball field. For protection, Skinny had learned to talk fast and to move fast, and he had developed an abiding interest in baseball, primarily because of the bat. When properly swung, a thirty-three-inch Louisville Slugger, he discovered, substantially improved many of his personal relations. By the time he had graduated from high school, Skinny had put on forty pounds, and among his other peculiarities and talents, he had developed into something of an anomaly: a fastball pitcher who could hit. Tulane University had offered him a baseball scholarship, and he had accepted it—a mistake that Skinny had recognized within the first week and that the university had finally rectified at the end of the second semester. Among the sons and daughters of privilege, Skinny had had no real frame of reference.

For one thing, except behind the cash registers and in the cafeterias' kitchens, there weren't any black people; and for another, the juvenile pranks and late adolescent rebellion characteristic of many of the students—the petty vandalism, purposely tattered new clothes, boisterous disregard of misdemeanor laws—were in the neighborhood Skinny came from exactly the things you fought hard *against*. So when one Friday late in the spring semester he had parked his car in front of a fraternity house, and that evening had returned after class and a late practice to find on it spilled beer, broken bottles, and an empty keg that had scratched the hood, Skinny had responded in a way that had brought a little slice of life in Gentilly to the genteel uptown neighborhood. One of the fraternity members had parked his Jeep on the yard in front of the house, and Skinny had unhesitatingly set to work on it with his bat, breaking out every piece of glass that was in it.

Accompanied by several of his brothers, the Jeep's owner had charged out onto the lawn and demanded that Skinny put down his bat and "fight like a man."

"Jesus Christ," Skinny had replied, his voice loud and nasal, swinging the bat cleanly and hard, stepping into it as if he were reaching for a low, outside curve. "You think you're still in grade school?"

The boy had jumped back just far enough that the very end of Skinny's bat had connected with his kneecap and knocked it right around to the side of his knee.

When the police had arrived a few minutes later, they had found Skinny still swinging, alternately pounding his bat against the Jeep's fenders and waving it in the air, talking the whole time, standing off at least a quorum of the assembled fraternity.

One of the policemen who worked the area—who had no fondness for the fraternity himself—had suggested to Skinny that, if he were a policeman, he could get paid rather than arrested for undertaking pretty much the same sort of labor, a suggestion that Skinny had not taken too seriously until, on indefinite expulsion from Tulane, he had learned that public service would get him an exemption from the otherwise inevitable Vietnam-bound draft.

So Skinny had become a policeman.

And the fact that he was now on suspension for the fifth time in his eleven-year career had in no way diminished his overall enthusiasm. The prospect of a cash reward didn't hinder him there, either. The only thing that did bother him, in fact, was why, if Stan Lee was really so anxious to find the person who had set the fire, he had been so reluctant to discuss the girl, dwelling instead on the lawyer who had made the offer to buy the building. As Skinny got back into his truck, he couldn't figure it, so he decided right then to find the girl first—he'd let Theriot handle the drone work.

*It's nice being a reasonable man,* Skinny thought, immediately pleased with the course he had set, thinking of the girl as she looked beside the pool, all greased up for the sun. *Then you can find a reason for anything.*

\*　　　\*　　　\*

The apartment complex Skinny lived in was made up of four three-story buildings arranged in a square. Between the buildings, in the large courtyard they formed, the swimming pool was surrounded by a broad concrete deck. On the deck were lounge chairs and small tables covered by big, beach-type umbrellas, and concrete planters filled with tropical plants. Access to the pool area was through the four corners of the square—the buildings didn't quite meet—and Skinny went in one corner and right back out another, not surprised to see that the girl was no longer there. He looked in the window of the complex manager's office before he went in, smiling brightly.

"Skinny's here," Skinny announced as he threw open the door, startling the woman who was alone in the office.

The complex manager's name was Marieth Mayeux, and she was certain that Skinny was the strangest skinny white man she had ever encountered.

Skinny was convinced that she liked him.

Marieth said, "You here about the report?"

"What report?" Skinny asked.

Marieth leaned forward and crossed her arms on her desk.

"Man was walking out by the pool, said he heard something sounded to him like a gunshot."

Skinny stopped to think that over for a moment.

"It must've been a car—" he began.

"That's what I said, too," Marieth interrupted him, looking right at him, her slightly bulging eyes magnified by her glasses, "but the man said no, wasn't no car—said it sounded to him like it had come from inside one of the apartments."

Skinny looked off, momentarily pretending to study a framed poster on the wall.

"You got any reports of *bodies?*" he asked, looking back. Before Marieth could reply, he added, "Then don't worry about it." He raised and dropped both his shoulders at once, and flashed a quick smile. "That's what you have Skinny for, right?"

Marieth moved some papers around on her desk, uncertain exactly what they had Skinny for.

"Skinny's got a favor to ask," Skinny went on. "He needs to see the rental application from a new tenant, but he only knows her first name."

"What is it?" she asked.

"Karen," Skinny replied. "She's short." Fingers together and palm down, he tapped one hand against his sternum. "About this tall. She drives a red car."

Without saying anything, Marieth pushed herself up from her desk and stepped over to a file cabinet, bent down, and began to go through it. When she found the file she was looking for, she stood up straight—and bumped into Skinny, who was standing right behind her, looking over her shoulder.

She turned in a way that forced Skinny to step back.

"You smell like you been medium-cooked," she said.

"Nah," Skinny replied, running his forearm along under his nose, sniffing himself, surprised at his own smokey smell. "Skinny comes rare." He took the file folder from her and quickly looked inside it.

Marieth went back to her desk.

The rental application was only one page, front and back, and other than a record of rent received, it was the only thing in the file. Skinny lifted the top page, dropped it back, began to read.

Karen had given her full name as Karen Kincaid Hodges, and according to the application, she had previously lived out-of-state. She had a checking account at a local bank and a ready-assets account at a local brokerage house, which Skinny knew meant she had at least ten thousand dollars invested in stocks—or at least she had had that much when she had opened the account. Under employer, she had written "self," and she had given her occupation as "developer." She had a cat named "The Butler." Her car had a local registration and license. Beneath the line on the form marked "For Office Use Only," Marieth had noted the dates she had verified Karen's accounts; and in a space marked "State/ NCIC" Skinny himself had initialed, indicating that he had run her name through the state computer and the National Crime Information Center, which almost certainly he hadn't. She had paid the damage deposit—two months' rent and an extra two hundred for the cat—in cash, and the two times she had paid rent, she had paid that in cash, too. She lived in a first-floor apartment.

"This is all you got?" Skinny asked, glancing up from the file.

Marieth had turned to her computer and didn't look away from the screen.

"That's it," she affirmed.

Skinny went to the small copy machine in the corner, copied the three pages, folded the copies and put them into his pocket, put the file on top of the file cabinet.

"Thanks," he said, and started out of the office.

"Thanks *again*," Marieth corrected him, the dry comment not interrupting the rapid click of the keys on her keyboard.

Skinny went outside, tapped on the window, and when Marieth looked up, made a face at her through the glass.

For almost five hours, until well after dark, every twenty minutes or so Skinny left his apartment and made a tour of the complex, going first around the parking lot then back in through the pool area, looking for some sign—her car or a light—that Karen had returned to her apartment. Between the first few orbits, he worked some more on his gun, without much success. Skinny felt certain that Karen's rental application was largely bogus, and the rent payments in cash intrigued him, too—what intrigued him most, however, was that, after she had lured Stan Lee out of his shop, Karen had apparently come right back to the complex to lie out in the sun.

*Either she's real dumb or she's very cool,* he thought, and either way—though he was sort of hoping for the former—he wanted to meet her.

After his first few tours of the area, Skinny became irritated with the interruptions to his work on his revolver, so he took to carrying it with him when he went outside, holding the cylinderless frame up close to his face, fooling with it as he walked, then stopping to look around; and he was doing just that when two things happened at once: Karen's car turned into the lot, and the revolver's rebound slide spring slipped out from under his thumb. The spring hit the front of a nearby car and bounced out of sight to his left. About forty feet to his right, Karen parked and pushed open her door. Skinny went both ways nearly at once, in rapid succession turning first toward the spring then back toward Karen, stopping there when he saw she was looking at him.

"Skinny lost his spring," Skinny said, explaining himself.

Karen did not say anything to that but looked at him strangely.

"You're Karen, right?" Skinny went on. "Karen Hodges?"

Karen was so short that, even in heels, only her face showed over the roof of her low-slung red car. At the mention of her name, however, she stepped forward, along the side of her car and up onto the curb, revealing herself fully.

She wore tight blue jeans with her high heels and a knit sweater-blouse that stretched just a bit to fit her. Her hips were high and round, tapered into a narrow waist, and the top of her was full and round, too. Even in the dim parking-lot light, Skinny could see that her eyes were bright blue. Her sun-streaked hair was straight, tucked behind her ear on one side, and fell down past her shoulders. Skinny was so taken by the sight of her up close that he almost forgot the sprung rebound slide spring.

"Skinny needs to talk to you," Skinny said, then he remembered the spring, stepped over to the car nearest him, and set the revolver down on the hood. He dropped onto all fours and began to look around on the ground near where he had seen the spring hit. "But he's got to find his spring before he does anything."

"Apparently," Karen remarked, and walked up beside him. "Aren't you the resident policeman?" she asked.

"That's Skinny," Skinny replied, glancing over his shoulder to look at her—looking up at her, she looked even better. "How'd you know that?"

"The manager described you—she said you'd be hard to miss." Karen put her large straw purse down on the car behind her. "What's the spring look like?"

"Like a spring," Skinny replied. He held his thumb and first finger an inch apart. "This long."

As Karen glanced around, she saw it, lying in the seam between the hood and fender of the car beneath which Skinny was looking. She picked up the spring and held it in her fist as she bent down beside him and pretended to look, too.

"What did you want to talk to me about?" she asked.

Skinny put both hands down flat and lowered himself to look all the way under the car.

"Stan Lee," he said, and pushed himself back up, then

turned on his knees to face her. He sat back on his heels and brushed his palms one past the other. "How'd you get mixed up with him?"

Karen sat down on the high curb.

"I'm not mixed up with Stan Lee," she replied, almost smiling, as if Skinny had asked something amusing.

Thinking about it, Skinny saw that it was sort of funny, trying to picture Stan Lee and her mixed up together. At close range, Karen was anything but the empty-headed blonde he had hoped for. She was self-possessed and confident, aware. Skinny could see that she knew the effect she had on men, but she was smart enough not to be coy about it, not to pretend the effect wasn't there. She was the sort of woman, he couldn't help thinking, who would let you know in a second exactly what *she* liked in bed.

*And why not?* he thought, thinking that if he looked as good as she did, he'd get a whole lot more of what he wanted, too.

"Call it what you want," he said, coming back to the point. "You went to see him this morning."

Karen drew up her knees and rested her arms on top of them.

"I thought I could deal with him better if I went to see him by myself."

Skinny's eyes flicked around, looking again for the rebound slide spring.

"Why did you have to deal with him at all?"

"I didn't, really," Karen replied. "It just seemed like a good idea." She tapped her fingers against her forearm, and momentarily, her eyes were vacant, fixed absently on the car next to her. When she looked back at Skinny, she saw that he was looking at her, his gaze calculating and very direct.

"A few months ago," she began, "I bought into a business.

What we do is, we buy properties and develop them. The warehouse district is very hot, and that's where we've concentrated—it's near downtown, and many of the buildings are vacant. A lot of people are tired of the suburbs. They're tired of mowing a lawn, and they're tired of commuting. They want a low-maintenance lifestyle, and they want to live near where they work. The market has a good, solid base."

Skinny couldn't say why, but as Karen explained her business—and what had led up to her meeting with Stan Lee that morning—he had the sense that she was trying to convince herself of something as much as she was just stating facts. He was curious about that and made a note to come back to it.

"We have two projects in the works now, and they're both doing well. So we're looking for something else in the same area—that's why we made the offers to buy the building Stan Lee and his partner were using for their shop."

"What would you do with it, assuming you get it?"

"We'd put retail space in the first-floor front and condominiums everywhere else."

"The lawyer who made the offers, he's your boss?"

"Partner," Karen corrected him.

Skinny accepted that.

"What's his name?" he asked.

"Grover Milham the third," Karen replied with a slight smile.

"Grover?" Skinny said sourly, as if he couldn't believe it. "You sure you haven't got your partner mixed up with his dog?"

"Positive," Karen replied, allowing her smile to broaden. "His dog's name is Muffin."

"Jesus," Skinny remarked, shaking his head. "I hope the poor bastard's not a Doberman."

"It's a schnauzer," Karen said, almost laughing.

Still shaking his head, Skinny lowered himself to the ground again, looking under the other car for his spring.

"So, anyway," Karen went on, "Grover went to see Stan Lee and Mitchell three times, trying to convince them to sell. Grover can be a charmer, but he wasn't having much luck with those two—"

"So you went to see them," Skinny concluded for her, his face near the pavement.

"So I went to see them," Karen affirmed.

Skinny craned his neck to look back at her.

"You probably should've gone in the first place."

Karen nodded agreement.

"I thought so, too," she said in a way that made it clear she had made the suggestion but had been overruled. She tapped her fingers against her forearm again. Her other hand remained closed in a small fist that Skinny only then noticed. "When Grover told me he was about to give up on them, I decided it was my turn. I got there early to catch them before their workday began, but Stan Lee was the only one in the shop."

Skinny rolled over, then sat up and leaned back against the door of the car on Karen's left.

"And you made a bet," he said, "who could make it across the Causeway the fastest."

Karen looked at him slyly.

"Right."

"You won?"

"Right again," Karen replied, obviously pleased with herself.

"So Stan Lee was ready to sell you the building, but when you got back, it was on fire."

"Maybe," Karen said, and tucked her hair back over her ear. "I don't know when the building caught fire. After the race, Stan Lee wanted breakfast. I dropped him off at the Hummingbird Grill and came home. I didn't hear about the fire until later."

"You still want the building, anyway, right?"

Karen nodded.

"Even more. It should be a bargain."

Skinny appeared to think that over for a moment, then he extended his right arm toward her, holding out his hand.

Without hesitation, Karen dropped the rebound slide spring onto his palm.

Skinny looked at the spring curiously before he looked back at her.

"All Skinny can say," Skinny said, "is that it's lucky for you you weren't racing Skinny."

Karen didn't think that over at all.

"You want to bet?" she asked, coming right back at him.

# 6

Rick Trask had panicked, and that bothered him. The knowledge of his own badly handled fear bothered him a lot, nagging at him, fueling his anger, which was more than considerable, anyway. It bothered him even more than the fact that there had been a man in the building Karen had guaranteed would be empty. For thirteen years, he had made his living from fires, and he had always been the steadiest man in the company, always thinking, the one they sent in when it got really hot; but he had run from this one like a little kid who had accidentally flared his father's can of gasoline.

He had run.

He was back in the office, one room up over a garage with a desk and three folding chairs, interviewing a prospective customer over the phone—just as he had been when he had first met Karen. The business was his idea, something he had convinced the guys of in the company: they could move furniture as a sideline on their time away from the station. All it took was a truck, and they sure as shit could use the extra money. *The Fireman's Carry*, he had called it.

"And the refrigerator?" he asked the woman on the phone, his anger barely concealed. "You want the refrigerator moved, too? How about the stove?"

On the best of days, Rick didn't have much patience with paperwork, but he knew he had to maintain the appearance that there was nothing wrong, nothing out of the ordinary going on; so he listened as the woman asked another question, wanting more assurances, right at the limit of his patience.

The UHF radio on the desk sounded suddenly, a routine report from a fire company leaving a scene—that had happened, too, when Karen had come in.

When he had first seen her, he hadn't paid much attention to her, and just because of her size he had thought that she was a little girl, lost somehow, maybe wandering into the office by mistake, maybe getting there just ahead of her mother. Then the radio had sounded, and she had moved closer to the desk to hear it: he had seen that she was little all right, but she wasn't anybody's little girl, not anymore, not in about fifteen years. Standing there in her tailored tan pants and dark blue silk blouse, heavy gold necklace showing beneath it, she had picked up the radio and had looked at it, studying it, holding it in a way that had made him picture her cute little manicured hands wrapped around his cock. Then she had looked right at him and smiled, her teeth very white next to her tan complexion, the one in front just a little crooked, making her look mischievous, as if she knew just exactly what he was thinking.

"What can I do for you?" he had asked.

"I'm moving," she had replied, and put the radio back in its charger, her smile still in place but becoming a little harder. "And I *like* fires."

"I like fires," Rick repeated to himself, and sat back in his chair, reiterating the obvious, the out he had given himself all along: Karen was the only person who could make him as an arsonist.

*And she* likes *fires,* he thought humorlessly.

"It'll be the best move you ever made," he reassured the woman on the phone.

Skinny had never seen so many gauges. The two big ones right in front of him, the speedometer and tachometer, they were pretty standard; but the others, the ones that ran along the dashboard, down the console, up between the sun visors, all glowing light blue or displaying light blue LED numbers, he didn't even know what half of them were. But he did know the feel of a big V-8 when it began to pull.

"Skinny feels like he's in an airplane," Skinny said happily, watching the tachometer, ready to shift.

Karen did not say anything to that but buckled her seat belt and put her elbow on the armrest, trying to appear more relaxed than she felt. Skinny had insisted on driving, saying it was only fair since she already knew the car and the drive to the Causeway would give him a chance to get the feel of it; and after she had given him the key, even before she had been able to go around to the passenger side and get in, he had had the engine started and revved up high, the stereo on then off again, and was asking her even as she opened the door whether or not she had insurance. Just getting out of the lot had been a trial. He had backed out of the parking space then accelerated, hard, while the wheel was still turned, so that he had had to spin the wheel left to avoid a parked car, then right to make the ninety-degree turn at the end of the lot, waving them around inside the car like seaweed caught in a rapidly changing current.

"Jesus," he had said, genuinely surprised that they had made it. *Out of the parking lot.*

That had slowed him down for about a block.

"Skinny likes your car," he had said when he stopped for a red light, smiling, flicking the switch and sending his window up and down, playing with it, Karen imagined, like an alien resident who had never before seen an electric window.

*Alien is the word,* she had thought.

"I like it, too," she had said dryly, but the message seemed not to have reached him.

"How do we work it?" he asked, on the expressway now, cruising along at ninety plus.

Karen pushed a button on the dashboard, and a large LED display jumped to 00:00. She pushed the same button again, and the stopwatch started, the half-inch-high numbers measuring their progress in hundredths of a second.

"You drive one way," she said. "I'll drive the other, and we'll time it."

Skinny glanced at the rapidly changing numbers then glanced back at the road.

"That's pretty simple," he said.

Karen pushed the button again and froze the display, noticing as she leaned back in her seat something that concerned her.

"Do you smell something burning?" she asked, looking around, not seeing any smoke but certain of the smell.

"You're probably smelling Skinny," Skinny offered, unconcernedly looking around with her.

"No, that's not it," Karen said. "I've *been* smelling you."

Skinny made a sour face, but he was beginning to register it, too. He backed off the accelerator and began to look in earnest.

Two of the instruments on the console went out suddenly. Then another.

Skinny glanced up. In the rearview mirror, he saw a car coming up behind them, and beside them there was a truck, blocking a move to the shoulder.

The first visible smoke puffed out from beneath the dashboard, followed almost immediately by a steady stream of it, dirty white and noxious.

"Shit," Skinny said. He had seen car fires before, and he knew that, once they got started, they flared up fast. He stomped on the gas, trying to get in front of the truck.

The truck sped up with them.

Karen drew back on her seat, pulling her legs in as yellow flames appeared behind the smoke, flickering under the dash.

Skinny braked then accelerated again; the truck stayed right beside them.

"Look at this joker," he said, his voice loud and nasal.

"What's he doing?" Karen asked, anger as much as alarm in her voice.

A single tongue of yellow flame flared over her side of the dashboard, then receded. The smoke looked like an inverted waterfall, flowing up, over the dash, acrid and irritating.

"Fuck this," Skinny said, his eyes burning, jamming the shift lever into second gear. "Hold onto your hat," he said, and he released the clutch and hit the brakes very hard. The car immediately began to skid, and he fought the wheel, pulling to the right, sliding, cutting in behind the truck.

The car behind them shot past, horn blaring, close enough to touch.

"Jesus," Skinny said, and jumped into the next lane without looking. "Get the windows open," he added, still braking hard, moving onto the shoulder.

"They won't work," Karen replied, stabbing at the buttons with her finger.

"Shit," Skinny said. He pounded the window on his side with the heel of his fist, feeling how solid it was, then tried the door, already knowing that it was locked, electrically locked, remembering how Karen had pointedly flipped the switch just after they had left the lot.

Yellow flames shot out, licking the dash, the smoke white and suffocating.

"You locked the doors," Skinny said.

"I *know* I locked the doors," Karen replied, and quickly lay back on her seat, starting to kick at her window, aiming the pointed high heel of her shoe at the glass.

They were hardly rolling now, hardly moving at all.

Skinny leaned down and began to feel along the floor, feeling the bright yellow flames right next to his face, trying to find something, anything, he could use to break a window. The carpet was hot to the touch, smoldering in places.

As Karen kicked, a chip appeared, then a shattered mosaic, then a small hole. Her heel hung up in the glass, and she squirmed around on the seat, trying to free it.

Skinny burned one hand before he felt the familiar shape of his cylinderless gun where he had put it on the floor. He grabbed it and burned his hand again.

"My foot's stuck," Karen said, squirming harder, her voice tinged with panic.

Skinny picked up the revolver by the grip and leaned right over her, then began to smash the silver barrel against the window, using both hands, hitting right beside her foot, holding his breath against the smoke, trying not to breathe.

The window shattered, and unhesitatingly he sprang right through it headfirst, taking the glass out with him, hitting the pavement hard, stunned but scrambling back to his feet, reaching back inside the car.

Karen twisted around, flailing, trying to find the release for her seat belt.

Skinny found it first, released it, then grabbed her, around the neck and under one arm, pulling her back through the window, stumbling as he did so, falling away from the car, keeping his feet only until he felt the grass on the far edge of the shoulder.

"Shit," he said as he fell and Karen fell on top of him.

She rolled right off.

Twenty feet away, bright yellow flames flared out through the shattered window in the car.

"I think you broke my ankle," Karen said.

# 7

The car had come to a stop about fifty yards from an overpass, and Karen and Skinny were sitting on the side of the grassy embankment that led up to it, watching firemen spray water into the still-smoking car. Behind and above them, cars roared past on the overpass; below and in front of them, a steady stream of cars went past slowly as the drivers crept along, looking at the burned-out shell of Karen's car on the shoulder of the expressway.

"Skinny's pissed off now," Skinny said. He was examining his silver gun, which somehow he had managed to hold on to, even after he had jumped through the window and pulled Karen from the car.

Karen glanced over at him.

"Skinny lost his spring again."

Karen had to smile at that, if only because she saw it, dangling from a thread on the front of his jacket. She reached over, plucked the spring from the thread, and handed it to him, watching as he saw what it was and began to smile.

"Thanks," he said brightly, and immediately set to work sliding the spring back into the frame. After a few moments, he had the spring replaced to his satisfaction, and he looked at Karen, studying her as she watched the firemen work.

Her hair was singed near the ends, and on one side her neck was red and raw where he had grabbed her. As far as he had been able to tell from feeling it, her ankle was sprained, not broken. Sitting there with one leg extended out in front of herself and the other leg bent, her expression sad and thoughtful, she seemed almost defeated; but Skinny didn't buy that for two reasons. First, he had seen the way she had reacted to the fire itself, more angry than fearful, kicking at the window hard and fast, not panicked at all, her short leg moving like a piston—he felt certain that, if he had not been in the car, she would have gotten out without him. And second, her eyes did not fit her expression. They were hard and alert, thinking but not necessarily thoughtful, not in the way her otherwise listless expression would suggest, anyway. The little wheels were turning in there, winding up to something, just as they had been since she had first sat down on the embankment.

"So who do you think did it?" he asked, pretending still to be fooling with his gun.

Karen shook her head slowly side to side, then rested her chin on her knee.

"I don't know," she replied, not looking away from her car.

For a moment, Skinny looked with her, seeing that, although the fire appeared completely out, the car continued to smoke. The glass had melted out of it, but the tires were still inflated and, overall, the body appeared surprisingly intact.

"It makes sense to Skinny," Skinny began, "that whoever set fire to Stan Lee's shop set fire to your car, too."

Karen did not seem very interested in Skinny's theory and said "Maybe" noncommittally, vaguely.

Skinny's green eyes locked on her.

"If Skinny were you," he said, "he'd get past the maybe stage pretty fast." He gestured toward the car. "He'd feel pretty sure somebody was out to kill him."

Karen reluctantly acknowledged that and leaned back, stretching out on her side, uphill on the grass.

"Maybe," she repeated. "Maybe it was the same person, but I don't think so—I think it was Stan Lee."

"Yeah? How'd he get to you so fast?"

"I don't know," Karen replied. "How did you?"

Skinny gave her that one.

"He seemed to know a lot about cars," she added.

Skinny was sitting slightly behind Karen, up a bit higher on the embankment, and from that angle, looking down through the armhole in her sweater, he was able to see nearly the whole side of her breast.

"Then the big question is, why would Stan Lee want to kill you?" he observed, hoping that Karen would not move to reply.

But she did, sitting up and turning at the same time, facing him and crossing her legs Indian-style. She winced when her sore ankle touched the ground, but she didn't move it. She sat forward so she wouldn't fall back.

"Do you know what a 'package' is?" she asked. "A real estate package?"

"How's Skinny going to know about real estate?" Skinny asked in reply, putting his silver gun down on the ground beside him. "He lives in an apartment."

"A package is several small parcels put together to make one big parcel," Karen answered her own question. "If you can consolidate the ownership of a big enough piece of land—a big enough 'package'—you make big developments possible, like a high-rise building or a shopping center."

"Yeah? So?" Skinny remarked, not exactly following her, uncertain how a real estate package related to her suspicions about Stan Lee.

"A package is much more valuable than the individual pieces that compose it," Karen persisted. "That's why there's so much maneuvering involved when you try to assemble it. If the owner of any one piece learns what you're doing, he can hold out for a huge amount of money, multiples of what his property is actually worth."

"So then you scrub the deal," Skinny interjected, "and tell that asshole to go jump in the lake."

"Sometimes that's *exactly* what you do," Karen agreed, smiling momentarily, "but most of the time, you can't."

"Why not?"

"Because you already have too much money invested to walk away from it. You've bought options and other properties, paid attorneys and accountants—maybe you've already developed a plan and arranged financing. And that all costs."

"So you're stuck, and you have to deal with the asshole."

"Right."

Skinny thought that over for a moment, putting it together with what he already knew.

"Stan Lee?" he guessed, doubtful of his own conclusion. "Stan Lee was holding out on you? Holding up your package?"

"Not *my* package," Karen quickly corrected him. "Grover's package." She plucked a weed from the grass and, using her thumbnail, began to strip away the outer layer of green. "Stan Lee wasn't holding out, he just didn't want to sell— for Grover, though, it amounted to the same thing."

"He was in a jam."

Karen nodded as she carefully peeled the outer sheath from the weed.

"Stan Lee had to know something was up when Grover kept coming back with better and better offers. Then I show up, and while he's out with me, his building burns down."

"With his partner inside it," Skinny added quickly, pointedly. "So why did he go after you? Why didn't he go after Grover?"

Karen shrugged as she studied the near-white pulp inside the stem, then she tossed the weed away.

"That's what I've been trying to figure out," she admitted. Her voice took on a speculative certainty. "I think he started with me because I was handier. Stan Lee is not the brightest man in the world. He's probably still sorting out what he suspects about Grover, but he *knows* I took him out of the building."

"Maybe," Skinny said doubtfully, and glanced off, down the embankment, in time to see a fireman coming up toward them. He started to stand up to see what the fireman wanted, but stopped when he felt Karen's hand on his knee.

"And I beat him," she said, looking right at him seriously. "I beat Stan Lee across the Causeway, and he was furious that he had lost to me."

Karen held his gaze for a long moment, then slipped her eyes away when the fireman called out, "Hey, Skinny."

"What?" Skinny replied irritably, still looking at Karen.

"I finally got your boy Theriot on the radio. He'll be here in a couple of minutes."

"Good," Skinny said. "Thanks."

The fireman just stood there, staring at Karen, his expression openly assessing and hungry, just this side of a leer.

"Get out of here," Skinny said when he noticed him, feeling as he said it Karen's I-told-you-so glance on him.

\*     \*     \*

The inside of the car had burned down to bare metal, and before they left, Karen, Skinny, and Mike Theriot stood near it as the tow-truck driver hooked up his truck to tow it away.

"You're lucky you got out of there," Mike Theriot said somberly, playing his flashlight over what was left of the interior. The dashboard was gone, burned right down to the fire wall. The steering wheel was a scorched, misshapen ring. All that was left of the seats was a mass of fire-blackened springs.

Neither Karen nor Skinny said anything to that but looked on as the tow truck's cable tightened and the car's front wheels left the ground.

They drove Karen back to the apartment complex, then waited in the unmarked police car as she limped on inside.

"That's one very sexy woman," Mike Theriot observed, not taking his eyes off Karen until she had closed her door.

"And smart," Skinny added. "Don't forget smart."

"You look at her," Mike Theriot went on, "and you think, sex. Then you feel like a child molester for even thinking it."

"She's in her mid-twenties," Skinny pointed out defensively.

Mike Theriot looked at him curiously.

"Yeah, but that's not the point. She's little. Even with her build, she still somehow looks like a little girl. You want to put your arm around her just to protect her, then you look a little closer, and you can picture her crawling all over you."

"So?" Skinny said, a little put off.

"So that's very sexy. You know the woman fifteen seconds and already you're picturing her in bed."

Aggravated, Skinny looked at Karen's apartment, then sat back in the corner formed by the back of the seat and the door.

"What did you find out about the lawyer?" he asked.

Mike Theriot seemed ready to say something but apparently thought better of it.

"Not much," he replied, just answering the question. He reached over to the backseat, opened his brown plastic briefcase, pulled out his clipboard. "His full name is Grover Villere Milham—"

"The third," Skinny added sourly.

"The third," Mike Theriot affirmed without comment. "He lives uptown, near Tulane—which is also where he went to college. His office is in the warehouse district, in a renovated building about three blocks from this morning's fire." He glanced up. "As opposed to this evening's fire. He's married, no kids. His secretary said he and his wife are both society types. Lots of Mardi Gras stuff, the zoo, the symphony—like that. He's also on the board of directors of the museum. He's forty-two years old."

"A pillar of the community, right?" Skinny said tiredly, rubbing his eyes using the heels of both hands. "What about his company?"

"Old and respected," Mike Theriot said. "It was started by his grandfather, and it's privately held, which means information about it is pretty hard to come by. They're developer-builders. They buy property and build something on it— condominiums, offices, apartments. Sometimes they sell what they build; sometimes they keep it."

"What have they built that Skinny's seen?" Skinny asked, unimpressed.

"A couple of things, probably," Mike Theriot said, and reached over the seat to drop his clipboard back into his briefcase. "But one thing for sure."

"Yeah? What's that?"

Mike Theriot waved his hand at the windshield.

"This apartment complex."

Skinny glanced appraisingly at the complex's brick facade and ran his tongue over his front teeth.

"Did they sell it after they built it, or do they still own it?"

"I think they still own it," Mike Theriot hedged, feeling a strange tension in Skinny and instinctively shying away from it. "I'd have to check."

Skinny slowly pulled one hand down his face, and said, "Grover owns Skinny's apartment," uncharacteristically quietly, not really out loud.

*Here we are again,* he thought, thinking of Karen and thinking of the time he had spent at Tulane, when the Grovers of the world had first come into his life. For a long moment, he resented them. He resented the advantages that had been given them—the companies, the portfolios, the practices already set up—and he resented the unearned ease of their lives.

*You screwed up,* he reminded himself. *Not them.*

"Yeah, but if they had backed Skinny down," Skinny asked himself, "would it have worked out the same?"

Skinny couldn't answer that one, but in quickly trying to reverse what had actually happened—putting himself in front of the dean of men with the big cast on *his* leg—somehow he caught a glimpse of himself dressed in a Grover-type uniform— in boat shoes, blue button-down shirt, and baggy khaki pants—and his good humor returned in a flash. He cocked his head to one side curiously.

"You think," he asked, "if Skinny puts Grover in jail, he'll go up on Skinny's rent?" He grinned, and Mike Theriot grinned with him, shaking his head. "So, anyway," Skinny went on, "did you get a key to Mitchell's room?"

Mike Theriot nodded.

"Yeah, and I've already been through it. It's pretty bleak. There's nothing there but some clothes, a bunch of girlie magazines, and a bunk."

"Skinny'd still like to see it," Skinny said, "but not tonight." He reached for the door handle and opened the door. "Skinny's going to bed."

Mike Theriot leaned forward and started the car, obviously in agreement.

"Call me at the office in the morning."

Skinny picked up his silver gun from the floor, then got out and pushed the door shut with his foot.

"Later," he said, seeing as he said it the light go off in the front window of Karen's apartment.

# 8

The next day, away from the bureau's office, Skinny met up with Mike Theriot and together they went to Mitchell's room over the Hummingbird Grill, which was, in fact, just as bleak as Mike Theriot had described it. Coming in through the dirty windows, the light was dingy gray. The floor was faded brown linoleum. For furniture, there was only a bare mattress on a steel bunk and a single wood chair; on the seat of the chair, there was a two-foot-high stack of glossy magazines that, after Skinny had thumbed through a few, put him in mind of nothing so much as anatomy textbooks dressed up here and there with odd scraps of transparent nylon. In the closet were a few old clothes in a pile on the shelf, and on the floor by the sink there was an old towel that Skinny didn't even want to touch with his boot.

"Let's get out of here," Skinny said, more than a little put off by the room, and from there they went to Grover's office, which was only three blocks away.

"That's it?" Skinny asked when he saw it, put off in a different way.

"That's it," Mike Theriot confirmed.

The blocky, three-story warehouse had very obviously been newly redone, painted a bright pastel pink, trimmed out with dark red and dark green. The regularly spaced windows were single, fixed-in-place sheets of dark glass. At street level, one corner had been cut off the old building, and between two dark green concrete columns, set back and at an angle to the curb, there was an entrance made up of the same dark-colored glass that had been used for the windows.

"What the fuck?" Skinny said, getting out of the car as Theriot went to park it and going on inside, knowing that he had to talk to Grover sooner or later and settling on sooner despite the way he was dressed.

Inside, the lighting was soft and indirect, reflecting off more pastel colors, and there was no one in sight. The gray carpet was dense without being thick. In the far corner was a receptionist's counter—not a desk—and on the walls there were big color photographs of projects that Grover had envisioned or built. When Skinny got tired of looking at the pictures of office parks and apartments, he went up to the counter, wondering where everyone was.

"Skinny's here," Skinny said, and rang the small bell that sat on a black rubber pad.

The woman who appeared behind the counter was bony and angular, and tall, almost as tall as Skinny. Her red-blonde hair was puffed out, sort of parted high on one side, so that she seemed to be peering out from behind it. Her face was long, finished with too square a jaw, but lively, filled with quick-witted good humor.

"Okay," she said, "so who's this Skinny?"

"This is Skinny," Skinny replied, and jabbed his forefinger against his own chest. "Who are you?"

"This is Ruth," Ruth said, mimicking Skinny's movement,

pointing at herself with one long, red-nailed finger. "What can Ruth do for Skinny?"

Skinny rolled his eyes before he looked back at Ruth and grinned in spite of himself.

"Jesus. Everybody's a comic."

Ruth smiled agreeably, showing her large, square teeth.

"Skinny needs to see Grover."

"Really? What does Skinny need to see Grover for?"

Skinny made a sour face and shifted his feet back so that he was leaning at a severe angle against the counter, pushing against it. Ruth had him off-balance, and she knew it.

"You're not making this easy."

Mike Theriot came up beside him.

"Oh, my," Ruth said. "Now there are two of you."

"There's only one Skinny," Skinny claimed quickly.

Ruth looked from Skinny to Mike Theriot then back again.

"So is he here or what?" Skinny asked before she could make another comment.

"Or what," Ruth replied.

"We're policemen," Mike Theriot interjected, and showed his ID.

Ruth thought that over, as if deciding whether or not to believe him. Momentarily, she chewed her lower lip thoughtfully, and in that moment, Skinny decided that he liked her. He liked the furrows that showed on her forehead and the seriousness behind the good humor in her eyes. He could see her in back somewhere, at her desk, that same thoughtful expression on her face, smoking a long, thin cigarette as she reviewed whatever it was she had just typed. There was something solid about her, solid yet fun. He looked to see if she was wearing a wedding ring, but she had leaned to one side and was reaching beneath the counter.

"Mr. Milham won't be in until this afternoon," she said as she stood up straight. "Why don't you come back then?" She placed two invitations on the counter. "We're having a party." She smiled. "See how much fun we're going to have?"

The invitation was black script printed on heavy white card stock and announced a press conference and cocktail party to celebrate Grover's most recent project, a plan to renovate yet another old warehouse.

"Oh, boy," Skinny said drily.

"Oh, boy," Ruth repeated, using the same tone.

"Hey," Mike Theriot exclaimed, still reading the invitation, "they got an open bar." He looked up expectantly. "And food."

Skinny gave him a sideways glance, then picked up his invitation and tapped one edge on the counter.

"You'll be here?" he asked Ruth.

"Ruth'll be here."

"Then Skinny'll be here, too."

From the corner in front of Grover's office, after a brief conversation, Skinny and Mike Theriot went off in different directions. Mike Theriot had to check in at the office, and Skinny wanted to try to find Stan Lee. Although Stan Lee had said that he didn't know exactly where he would spend the night, Skinny suspected that he wouldn't stray far from his shop, despite its present condition. At any rate, the shop was the only place he knew to look for him, so he walked back the way he and Mike Theriot had come earlier, in the direction of the Hummingbird Grill.

The day was clear but warm, and Skinny walked more slowly than he usually did, surveying the starkness of the warehouse district, which was made up almost completely of concrete and brick. There were several things bothering him that he couldn't quite understand. According to Karen, Grover had the most to gain from the fire that had killed Mitchell, yet she was convinced that it was Stan Lee who had set fire to her car. And in a way that made sense. Stan Lee was *not* the brightest man in the world, and Skinny knew he'd know more about Grover when he found out how much he had actually invested in the "package." Still, there was something about that sequence that seemed just a bit too neat, and Skinny couldn't help feeling that something was missing, some big piece he should already see.

At the door to the shop, Skinny shrugged in his characteristic way, raising and dropping both his shoulders at once, for the moment dismissing his doubts, and ducked under the bright yellow crime-scene tape.

The embers crunched beneath his boots as Skinny walked around the ground floor of the warehouse, idly trying to picture what had happened. He studied the junction box and the rearranged wires, but he didn't really know enough about wiring to know what he was studying, so he left there to reexamine the scorched five-gallon bucket of glue. After a few seconds of that, because he had already been through the office, he went on upstairs, testing his weight on each step of the badly burned stairs.

The second floor had burned through in places, and along the edges of the holes, the heavy wood flooring was blackened and cracked. Overhead, there was a gaping hole in the roof; sunlight streamed in, showing on surfaces that hadn't seen direct light in a hundred years. A smokey, burned, wet smell was pervasive. Skinny walked carefully, up on the balls of his feet, looking around at the various stacks of wood and supplies that littered the large space, and occasionally glancing out the large windows. Behind a stack of plywood, he found what appeared to be a path that led between old tools and appliances, boxes of wood scraps, and even assorted furniture, and he followed it until he found the place where he felt certain that Stan Lee had spent the night.

Near the back wall of the warehouse, a cardboard carton had been split open and laid out flat on the floor. Beside it, there was an empty can of Spam, a box of Saltine crackers, and six empty red and white cans of Budweiser, one of which had been used as an ashtray. A yellow sports shirt was wadded up as a pillow.

Suddenly, Skinny had the unsettling sense that he was intruding, intruding in a dangerous way, as if he was disturbing an only temporarily vacated lair.

He glanced around quickly but saw nothing move.

The beer cans were arranged in a row.

Tucked under one edge of the cardboard, almost hidden, there was a three-by-five color photograph. Skinny glanced around again, and listened, before he stepped forward to pick it up, seeing as he lifted the edge of the cardboard other photographs in a stack, farther in. He picked up the loose photograph and the stack, then stood up.

In the top picture, although she appeared to be driving, Karen was looking right at the camera, her blue eyes annoyed yet excited, her blonde hair blowing out behind her. Judging from the way her lips were pursed, she seemed about to say something, something terse, Skinny thought, quickly putting the picture of Karen together with where he had found it, realizing the photographs had been taken during Karen and Stan Lee's race across the Causeway.

The next picture was centered on her chest. Wind was ruffling the front of her blouse, lifting it away from her body, and beneath a gold necklace one breast was completely exposed, soft and white, contrasted by the line of her tan. Farther down, her tight jeans encased the swell of her hips and her thighs as she sat, legs slightly apart to work the pedals.

"Jesus," Skinny said, and began to flip through the rest of the photos.

There were several more pictures of Karen—though none so revealing as that first one—and there was a strangely empty picture that showed only the sleek, red hood of her car sloping down to the Causeway's concrete roadway, the broad, gray expanse of Lake Pontchartrain in the background. Interestingly, there were also a half dozen pictures of the front of the shop, before the fire, that appeared to have been taken at different times of day. In one, the early sun was behind the building, the facade in deep shadow, and in another, the inside lights were already on.

Skinny came back to the picture of Karen's torso and was studying it in detail, holding the picture up close to his face, when he heard a faint rustling sound behind him. He started to turn to see what it was, but he felt a cool, sharp pressure behind his ear, like a small, round cookie cutter—or the barrel of a twelve-gauge shotgun—digging into his scalp.

He heard Stan Lee say, "Freeze right there, peckerwood," in a flat, murderous twang that made his blood run ice-cold.

"Jesus Christ, Stan Lee," Skinny almost shouted, starting badly, "no one says peckerwood."

He felt the sharp pressure removed from behind his ear, and he turned to see Stan Lee standing not three feet away, holding a length of three-quarter-inch pipe.

"I thought you might'a been one of them looters," Stan

Lee explained sheepishly, though obviously amused, smiling slightly.

Skinny just glared at him.

"A man has to be careful in the city," he added earnestly.

Stan Lee's hair was disheveled, falling in greasy strings across his forehead, and he ran one big, bony hand through it, pushing it back.

"I guess I should put on my glasses."

Stan Lee was wearing the same baggy blue jeans Skinny had seen him in the day before and a ribbed white undershirt that exposed an ugly, star-shaped scar on his shoulder. He saw Skinny look at the scar, and said, "I was in a bad car wreck."

"It looks like you were shot," Skinny countered sharply, his tone leaving no doubt that he was more than a little perturbed.

A slow grin creased Stan Lee's face.

"That's what I tell the ladies," he said.

Stan Lee put the pipe in his hip pocket, then walked across the cardboard that was spread out on the floor. He sat down, reached between two packing crates, and took out a pair of brown, lace-up shoes.

Skinny knew that Stan Lee had startled him purposely, but as he watched him remove his thin brown socks from inside the shoes and put them on, he decided for the moment to just let it go.

"So, Stan Lee," he began as Stan Lee put on his shoes, "where did you get these pictures?"

"I took 'em," Stan Lee replied without looking up. "The girl had a camera and told me I could."

"You did pretty well with it," Skinny observed, and glanced again at the full-color picture that featured Karen's chest.

"It's one of those automatic things—all you have to do is press the button."

Stan Lee finished tying his laces and stood up.

"I still have it."

"What?" Skinny asked. "The camera?"

Stan Lee nodded.

"I took it when I got out of her car, didn't think I still had it."

Skinny stopped looking at the picture of Karen and shifted his gaze to Stan Lee.

"Skinny can understand that," he said thoughtfully, tapping the stack of photographs against the open palm of his hand. "You were upset, right? Since she had just won the race?"

Stan Lee didn't rise to that as much as Skinny had hoped.

"It wasn't a real race," he replied. "I told you that. She was running a game on me, getting me out of the building so her friends could come in and set it on fire."

"So you set her car on fire to get even."

Stan Lee bent down and picked up his shirt.

"I don't know nothing about no car fire."

"Karen thinks you do. She says she *knows* it was you."

"That bitch don't know shit," Stan Lee snapped, his voice flat and hard. He pulled on his shirt with a barely restrained violence. "She thinks she's so fucking cute, sashaying on in here, twitching her ass around her rigged deal, and within a hour my business is burned down and my partner is dead." He jammed his shirttail down into his jeans. "That's what *I* know."

"Calm down, Stan Lee," Skinny said easily, smiling himself. "Skinny's just giving you a hard time."

Stan Lee fixed his pale, almost colorless eyes directly on Skinny. After a moment, the slow grin again creased his face.

"I guess you owed me that one," he said.

"I guess I did," Skinny replied.

Stan Lee finished tucking in his shirttail, glanced around, started along the path that lead back to the stairs.

"Where are you going?" Skinny asked.

"I got things to do," Stan Lee replied.

Skinny went after him, almost immediately snagging his field jacket on a box filled with scrap. He freed himself and caught up to Stan Lee at the top of the stairs.

"I got to see about my insurance," Stan Lee continued, "and I got to get some new clothes." He put his hands in the hip pockets of his jeans, palms flat against his hips, and for a long moment he stared blankly down the long flight of stairs, his pale eyes vacant yet moving, changing focus away then back, as if he were seeing someone climbing the stairs. "And I got to make arrangements for Mitchell's funeral." He moved onto the first step. "You wait here until I'm all the way to the bottom."

Skinny nodded agreement, having no desire himself to find out whether or not the burned stairs would hold two people; and as he idly watched Stan Lee, moving slowly, as if he were hobbled, it occurred to him suddenly to ask himself despite his aversion to the man personally, what if Stan Lee was telling the truth? What if he had *not* set the fires—either the warehouse fire or the car fire? Then, working backward, the most important question became the same one Stan Lee had wanted answered first: not who had arranged the fires but, who had actually set them? That was, Skinny saw, the missing piece.

*Brilliant*, he thought, and for a few moments, at least, he wasn't exactly certain what to do with the new possibility.

# 9

At home that afternoon, Skinny wandered around his apartment, disturbingly unsettled. He knew he really should wear a coat and tie to the party at Grover's office, and that bothered him. It wasn't so much the coat and tie itself, of course, as it was what it meant to him: the last time he had voluntarily put on a tie was for a university-sponsored dinner in his first semester at Tulane, and that occasion had worked out poorly at best, when his white socks, white shoes, and matching white belt had proved not to be quite as stylish as he had first thought. So as he showered, then dressed in a dark gray suit and knotted a quiet red tie, he was already perturbed; and when his doorbell rang, he just about yanked the door off its hinges pulling it open.

"What?" he said irritably before he saw who it was.

Karen stood out on the walkway, looking up at him. Her bright blue eyes quickly took in the suit and the tie.

"Wow," she said. "Who are you?"

"Feast your eyes now," Skinny replied. "You won't see Skinny like this too often."

For her part, Karen was dressed in a beige silk dress with a very narrow brown belt that matched her shoes. The top of the dress was cut similarly to the blouse revealingly ruffled in Stan Lee's pictures; and the same gold necklace glinted along the line of the delicate material in a way that made Skinny recall the line of her tan.

She held up a bottle of champagne.

"I stole it," she said proudly. "They'll be one bottle short at the reception."

"You're going?" Skinny asked dumbly.

"Of course I'm going," Karen replied.

"How did you know Skinny was going?"

"Because it's *my* party. I put it together." She handed him the bottle of champagne. "And because Ruth told me she had given you an invitation."

Skinny glanced at the label on the bottle, then glanced back at Karen.

"Skinny'll get some glasses," he said.

Karen followed him into the apartment, into the kitchen, and leaned against the counter, which caught her rib-high.

Skinny took down two unmatched glasses, unwrapped the cork on the champagne, then popped it, bouncing it off the ceiling. He poured champagne into the glasses until they were full, watching it foam up then settle.

"You need a ride, right?" he guessed.

Karen nodded as she sipped, holding her glass with both hands.

"Right." She glanced at her watch. "And I have to be there pretty soon."

"What's the story on your car?"

Karen put her glass down on the counter, then adjusted her narrow belt, aligning the buckle with the buttons on the top part of her dress by sliding the belt in back.

"I was hoping you would tell me," she replied. "*You* still have it."

"Skinny hasn't got it."

Karen put one hand on her hip.

"The police still have it, and you're one of them."

"Skinny's Skinny," Skinny said matter-of-factly. "He's not one of anything."

Karen appeared about to comment on that but picked up her champagne instead.

"You're certainly different," she agreed, glancing at him playfully out of the corners of her eyes.

Skinny made a sour face that turned into a reluctant smile. Three swallows into it, he was already feeling the champagne, feeling the beginning of a pleasant buzz. When Karen glanced again at her watch, he said, "Let's get moving," and with his free hand picked up the bottle.

Karen nodded emphatic agreement and quickly turned to go. She started forward, then stopped abruptly to leave her glass on the counter.

Skinny, who had started forward with her, bumped into her.

"Sorry," he said, and before he could step back, Karen turned. With the front of his thigh he felt material slide, a sexy glide of silk over slick panties beneath.

For a provocative fraction of a second, Karen did not move away; then she started again for the door.

When a moment later Skinny went after her, he tried to flap his arms in his characteristic show of enthusiasm, but with the bottle of champagne in one hand and the glass of champagne in the other, his range of expression was seriously diminished.

\*　　　\*　　　\*

At Grover's office, in the large reception area Theriot and he had visited earlier, Skinny stood leaning back against the receptionist's counter in the corner, drinking a VO and water with a wedge of lemon that he hadn't wanted, surveying the party which, an hour and a half into it, seemed to have just reached its peak. Karen and he had arrived a few minutes before the first guests, and for a while there it had been fun, being the first to the bar and to the buffet tables, sampling the boiled shrimp and the three different sauces, the lump crabmeat on crackers, the oysters prepared so many different ways he had finally lost track. But when more guests had arrived, Karen had gone off, and Skinny had been left to his own devices, which in this situation were not very clever: he ate shrimp until just the sight of them made him move away from the table, he drank a lot of VO, and he surreptitiously watched Karen.

She moved effortlessly about the large, crowded room, entering into glib conversation with the small groups that had formed, then a few minutes later, leaving just as easily to move on to another. After a while, Skinny could discern the nuances of her obviously well-practiced greetings—the touch on the arm, kiss on the cheek, or firm and direct handshake, the warm, radiant smile or exaggerated concern, the way she looked men squarely in the eye and tactfully deferred to the women—and although he knew she was working and that, in fact, so was he, still he felt clumsy and excluded, and what was worse, out of place. As he drank more, he became more and more unreasonably uncomfortable until he had all but decided to leave, when he felt a light touch on his own arm.

"So Skinny made it," Ruth said.

She was nearly as tall as he was, and even her loose, flowery dress could not hide her long-boned angularity. She held a drink in one hand, and a long, thin cigarette in the other. She looked tired, tired but still in good humor.

"Skinny made it," Skinny said.

"Nice suit," Ruth added, with just a trace of mischief.

Skinny gave her a pained look.

"Skinny would rather be fishing," he said.

"Ruth would rather be fishing, too," Ruth admitted, reaching past him to tamp out her cigarette in the ashtray on the counter. That done, she turned so she could survey the crowd with him, her hazel eyes watchful but dispassionate.

"You know all these people?" Skinny asked.

"I know who most of them are," Ruth replied, carefully making the distinction.

She tucked in her chin as she glanced around, and a crease appeared in the skin on her throat, beneath the line of her jaw. She angled her drink slightly to indicate the two men in a cluster nearby.

"There's a prominent French Quarter property owner having a chuckle with the director of the Vieux Carré Commission. They look awfully friendly, don't they?"

Without looking at Skinny, she angled her glass again.

"The man whispering to the woman in red, he's the head of the Arts Center. She's one of the Center's big benefactors— she's a Claiborne, you know. Her family came over just after Bienville founded our fair city."

Skinny's glance followed Ruth's.

"She looks old enough to have founded a city herself," he said.

Ruth smiled appreciatively.

"Which one is Grover?" Skinny asked, while she was still smiling.

Ruth's smile faded quickly, and her eyes flicked over the crowd then stopped at a point near the center buffet table.

"Just follow the bouncing blonde," she replied, her tone surprisingly dry.

Skinny glanced at her curiously before he glanced back at the crowd, in time to see Karen join two men in a large group.

"Grover is the shorter of the two," Ruth added, excluding Karen.

Grover was short, all right, not over five-five, and he was handsome in a boyish sort of way, saved from cuteness by small, quick eyes that looked out past a nose that was slightly too large for his face. His sandy brown hair was tousled slightly, in a way that complemented the cut of his stylish Italian suit. When Skinny first spotted him, he was gesturing extravagantly, throwing one loose-wristed hand up by his shoulder, wrapping his other arm across his middle, chewing as he spoke then quickly wiping his mouth with a wadded-up paper napkin. The people around him were laughing, obviously amused by what he was saying, and he was just as obviously playing right to them, becoming more expansive as they laughed even harder—all but the man on his right.

"Who's the other man? The one who's not laughing?"

"He never laughs," Ruth observed before she answered the question. "That's Morgan Barrett—he and Grover are partners."

Skinny took a swallow of his drink, looking over the rim of the glass at the group. Morgan was taller than Grover but less colorful, staid and businesslike in his dark-suited presence.

"And Karen is a partner, too?" Skinny asked.

Ruth glanced at Skinny with a thin tolerance that revealed a suppressed anger.

"There are partners, and there are partners. Some are more equal than others." When Skinny seemed puzzled by that, she explained, "Morgan Barrett is big money. This"—she waved her hand in a way that indicated the whole office—"is just *one* of his businesses. It's Grover's *only* business, and Karen, no matter what she wants to believe, is only a small part of Grover's only business."

Ruth had been looking right at Skinny, but suddenly she looked away, apparently embarrassed by her own vehemence.

Skinny pretended not to notice.

"They look like they've known each other a long time," he said, pointing at the group by straightening one finger, uncurling it from his drink.

Ruth picked up the ashtray and put it within easy reach.

"Why do you say that?" she asked.

Skinny shrugged as he drained the rest of his drink, then fished out the soggy wedge of lemon.

"They *have* known each other a long time," Ruth affirmed.

She reached into the pocket of her dress and came out with a single cigarette, which she lit right away with a thin butane lighter.

"Morgan and Karen went to prep school together, up east." She exhaled smoke through her nose. "Morgan and Grover met in college—"

"At Tulane," Skinny interjected, using his teeth to tear off a piece of the lemon. "Skinny went there, too."

Ruth gave him a surprised look.

"Skinny wasn't there long," Skinny said, closely examining the lemon, planning his next bite. "It didn't take."

"Why not?" Ruth asked, very obviously curious.

Skinny used his front teeth to scrape the pulp from the peel.

"Too much inbreeding," he said, making a face at the sour taste of the lemon. He gestured at the far side of the room. "It makes people short."

Ruth grinned at that and looked away, again surveying the crowd.

Skinny put the gnawed remains of the lemon in his glass and put the glass on the counter. He was interested in what Ruth had just told him, though he wasn't exactly certain what to do with the new information. Karen and Grover and Morgan looked cozy, all right, but Karen had already pointed a finger at Grover—and who knew what else would develop when he figured out how to turn up the heat?

He glanced at Ruth speculatively, his shrewd eyes assessing and curious.

Across the room, two things happened at once: Mike Theriot arrived late and went straight to the nearest buffet table; and Grover mounted a small dais.

"May I have your attention?" Grover called. He waved one hand over his head, then used that same hand to brush his hair from his forehead, pushing it off to one side. "May I have your attention, please?"

Slowly, the room quieted.

Mike Theriot did not look up from the shrimp.

Grover said something that made the people nearby laugh, unbuttoned and rebuttoned his double-breasted coat, looked out at the hushed crowd.

"First of all," he began, "I'd like to thank you all for coming." He put his left hand in his pants pocket. "In these health-conscious times, it does my heart proud"—he placed his right hand casually over his heart—"to see how many people will still come out for a little free booze."

"Cheap booze, at that," a woman called.

"It's not cheap booze, either," Grover protested amidst the outbreak of laughter. "And by now, Miss Cici Claiborne, *you* should know the difference."

Skinny looked again at the old woman Ruth had pointed

out to him a few moments before and saw that she was laughing heartily, delighted to have been mentioned by name. She whispered to the man next to her, then laughed again.

"A lot of people are tired of the suburbs," Skinny heard Grover say, beginning his presentation, and when he looked back to the front of the room, he saw Grover reading from cards—and Ruth right behind him. Skinny glanced needlessly to his left, surprised to see that she was not still where she had been.

"They're tired of commuting," Grover went on, "and God knows, they're tired of mowing a lawn. People today want a low-maintenance lifestyle, and they want to live near where they work."

Skinny knew those words. He knew he had heard those same words before, but just then he did not bother to recall where because he was busy watching Ruth, watching as she moved around the small dais, preparing for Grover's presentation. First, she rolled a tall cart with a slide projector on it out into the crowd, then she took a long extension cord and plugged it into the wall. She moved to a row of switches and worked them, unfurling a projection screen that dropped down from the ceiling, dimming the lights, then she went back to the projector and turned it on. There was something about her movements that bothered Skinny, something that disturbed him in a strange way, but it wasn't until Grover held out his hand for the projector control—and Ruth was right there to put the device in his hand—that he knew what it was.

"The market in the warehouse district has a good, solid base," Grover said, and worked the projector control, pointing to the screen as the first image appeared.

It was done well, Skinny acknowledged, the way Ruth had prepared the equipment and how Grover used it, smoothly backing up his assertion with a bright, colorful graph; and in that one contiguous motion—in that moment when Grover held out his hand, knowing the control would be there, the preparations already made, the image appearing, like magic, just when he wanted it—Skinny had seen what it meant to have money. Suddenly, he understood the presumption.

Ruth adjusted the projector and brought the graph into sharp focus.

More than the ownership of things, Skinny saw, to have money was to make presumptions: to presume that you got what you wanted just when you wanted it. Money made the small details of life—the duties and necessities that occupied people without money most of their lives—almost completely disappear. That was what he saw in the way Grover had reached for the projector control, all the meals and drinks he had accepted in the same manner, the cars kept clean and well running, the neatly mown lawns, clean houses, trips arranged in advance. To a lesser extent, he now saw the same thing in Karen—and he had definitely seen it in the fraternity boys who had scratched up his car. They had presumed that, at worst, a few dollars would take care of whatever damage they did, and it was small wonder, then, that they had not known what to do other than to call the police when Skinny had taken out payment in kind.

"Fight like a man," they had told him, which Skinny now saw meant, "Play by *my* rules."

"Fuck that," Skinny said to himself, remembering how he had kept swinging his bat.

The projector flashed, and on the screen another graph appeared, just as bright as the first.

"We have two projects in the works now," Grover said, "and they're both doing well."

"So we're looking for something else in the same area,"

Skinny said before Grover did, suddenly remembering how Karen had said exactly those words when he had first spoken to her in the parking lot.

"And now we're ready to start up a third," Grover continued. "Negotiations have been difficult, but only this afternoon we committed to the property we really wanted."

The projector advanced again, and there was a full-frame picture of Stan Lee, grinning sheepishly for the camera, showing the too-white caps on his teeth, looking for all the world like the cracker he was.

"The former owner," Grover remarked to lighthearted chuckles. "And the property itself," he added, and clicked the projector again.

There was more laughter when the next slide appeared, an unflattering, black-and-white news photo of Stan Lee's shop that had been taken just after the fire. In the picture the old warehouse was still smoking and looked like something left over from World War Two.

*Now show how the man looked who died in the fire,* Skinny thought with a righteous anger he did not really feel. *See if that gets more laughs.*

"Of course we plan some improvements," Grover said.

"All it'll take is a lot of money," Skinny finished for him, the righteous anger transforming, becoming a bitterness he really did feel.

# 10

After Grover had finished his presentation, after Ruth had returned the lights to their normal brightness, Karen had seen Skinny leave. She had seen him speak briefly with the other policeman, Mike Theriot, and before that she had seen him talking to Ruth. She had, of course, noticed that he had stayed in the corner after the party had picked up, not mingling at all with the other guests, not even trying to fit in; but still it surprised her when he left so abruptly, without even saying good-bye, an unexpected event she replayed to herself as she got undressed and got ready for bed.

She kicked off her shoes near the door to her closet and dropped her dress in a heap right beside them.

Not that it mattered all that much, really, she figured, as she sat on the corner of the bed to peel off her stockings. In a way it even made things much easier. The next time she saw him, she would express irritation that he had left her stranded without a ride home, which would put him on the defensive, a posture he could not overcome without making some small concession. Since she did not need that much from him, it was, she knew, all the edge that she needed.

She left the stockings, inside out, on the floor beside the bed, stood up, and went into the bathroom.

Morgan Barrett, however, was not nearly so simple a problem.

The sink was high enough for her that she could, without leaning too much, rest an elbow on the counter as she brushed her teeth, figuring how to play Morgan as she did so.

Karen had met Morgan Barrett at the Phillips Exeter Academy, the prep school they had both attended in New Hampshire. Even though Morgan was two years ahead of her, because they were both from New Orleans, they were soon introduced and developed an acquaintance they both were quick to exploit. Morgan did not fit in well at Exeter. He was neither an athlete nor a scholar, and he did not trouble to be either outgoing or particularly eccentric. Until Karen came along, he was not so much an outcast as he was thoroughly unnoticed; but during his upper and his senior years, he became very popular just because he knew his new friend, who at fifteen years old was almost completely developed physically, a fact that went anything but unnoticed by the six hundred teenaged boys sequestered through long, hard winters outside a remote New Hampshire village. For her part, Karen found in Morgan an unthreatening, convenient entree into the upper classes of boys who were of much greater interest to her. By the time Morgan graduated and went on to Tulane, Karen had become an upper herself. When she graduated and went on to college in Virginia, during her frequent visits to New Orleans, their acquaintance was renewed. Karen visited Morgan when, say, she wanted to go to a certain party or to be seen at the right place for lunch, and Morgan allowed himself to be used because he still enjoyed the attention she brought him. And the form of their relationship was solidly fixed until Karen discovered she would not inherit much money—not enough, anyway, to last her the rest of her life.

"You can always come to work for me," Morgan offered.

They were at Commander's Palace, in the Garden Room, at a table by the big windows. Outside, dense early afternoon sunlight filtered down through great live oaks. Inside, the air-conditioned air was as crisp as the starched white tablecloths on the tables.

"It's not like I'm destitute," Karen protested, already regretting that she had told him anything at all. Her father had died suddenly six weeks before, leaving a smaller-than-expected estate that would, Karen had learned, be divided up about equally among his three ex-wives, three children, and, of course, the six separate lawyers.

"No one claimed that you were," Morgan replied. Using his fingers, he picked a piece of lump crabmeat from his salad, popped it into his mouth, and chewed slowly, savoring the taste.

Karen very nearly got up and left because she saw right away that it wasn't just the lump crabmeat he was savoring but her change in status. She was stung by the realization that she might in the future actually have to go to work—and how that would affect her whole life.

"That's very good," Morgan added.

He looked out the window, his eyes drooping contentedly as he continued to chew, the motion of his jaw only partially concealing a badly suppressed smirk. When he looked back, he found Karen's blue eyes fixed on his in an angry, rock-steady stare.

"I'll have some money to invest," she said, knowing that

he would likely try to take whatever money she gave him.

"I'll look around," he replied, smiling thinly, "and see what I can find."

Karen washed her face and applied lotion before she pulled on the large T-shirt she used as a nightgown. Before she left the bathroom, she turned out the light.

What Morgan had failed to anticipate, Karen knew, was just how seriously she would play the game they had entered into. That was her edge, the fact that she would do anything to keep her money and to add to it. Anything. As she saw it, she had to. It had taken her a while to figure out what Morgan was up to when he had had Grover offer her a piece of the property they owned in the warehouse district, but she had accepted because she had finally seen through his plan and had come up with a scheme of her own. She was certain Morgan did not know of the package she had assembled—or what it meant to her that she had a buyer. But since Stan Lee had signed over his shop, just as she had guessed that he would, she was that much closer to letting him know, a victory she allowed herself to envision as she got into bed and turned off the light.

With the final piece now in place, Karen would enter into an agreement with her buyer, committing to sell the whole package she had assembled. The sale price was fair, even good. Both Morgan and Grover would make money—that much was unavoidable. But rather than take a commission from the sale, Karen had reserved for herself the role of exclusive leasing agent for the entire retail complex her buyer would build, a role that guaranteed her a huge annual income for at least fifteen years. All she had to do now was to divert the blame for the fire, throw up enough smoke of her own that no firm conclusion could ever be reached.

She got up from bed, remembering to set her alarm.

She wasn't sure which pleased her more, the guaranteed income or how she had gotten it, using Morgan and using *his* money, rather than the other way round.

*That's strange,* she thought, seeing that her alarm clock was not working, though she was sure she had glanced at the time when she had first gotten in. But the bright red numbers were no longer glowing, that much was for certain. She picked up the clock, tried the switches in back, then tried to turn on the lamp.

The lamp didn't work, either.

She put down the clock and looked around in the darkness, wondering what was the matter, deciding what to do next, when she heard a faint snick of metal on metal that made fear shoot right up her spine.

Blood rushed in her ears, and for several seconds she was unable to move, even to breathe, and she heard another sound even more frightening than that first one, the sound of glass cracking, muffled somehow, splitting quietly.

Something in her seemed to take over, to make her move, and suddenly she was going very fast, fast but quietly, out of the bedroom, down the short hall, into the living room before she realized she was not moving away from the sound but toward it, the rough scraping sound of glass being gently removed.

In the darkness she saw the drapes sway, the heavy drapes over the sliding glass door that led out to the patio. Gray light in a thin strip showed beneath them, appearing to pulse as the drapes rocked, back and forth.

She ran to the front door and twisted the knob, with her other hand feeling for the key she always left in the dead-bolt lock, for a fraction of a second not finding it, not knowing where else to look.

Behind her, she heard the distinctive click of the lock in the sliding glass door, the short lever moved upward.

She found the key and twisted it, one way then the other, frantically pulling on the knob until the door came open, and she slipped through it, running away a few steps then quickly going back, pulling the door closed before she ran off again.

Skinny had been perturbed by Grover's party, no doubt about it, but he had gotten over it in less time than it had taken him to shoot three games of pool—which had taken almost no time at all. After he had left Grover's office, on the way home he had impulsively exited the expressway in Gentilly and gone to visit the neighborhood where he had been raised—and where his parents still lived. The lights were off in his parents' house, which, he knew, meant that they had already gone to bed, so for a while he had just driven around, going past the old corner grocery, the middle school, the ball field where he had first learned to play baseball. The houses, he noticed, were small, narrow in front and set close together. Cars—some derelict but most still serviceable—were parked on both sides of the street. There were almost no trees.

After a few minutes, Skinny started to leave his old neighborhood, to go on home, but on the way back to the expressway he saw the red-neon sign in the window of the local pool hall; and he decided before he left to shoot a few games of pool. The pool hall was no bigger than it looked from the outside, hardly big enough to accommodate the three side-by-side tables and narrow bar on one wall. Skinny put money down on the center table, ordered a draft beer, went back to the table, racked the balls, and began to shoot.

Skinny could shoot pool, any game, even billiards. There

was something about the vectors involved and the strategy
he could instinctively see. There was something about it he
felt, the proper stroke of the cue, the precise rolling weight
and force of the cue ball that resulted. One long arm bent at
the elbow, bent at the waist, his long, skinny legs placed
apart for stability, the sharp angles in his position often
seemed to match the angles of the shot he was getting ready
to take. On the first run, he sank eleven balls in a row.
He reracked, broke again, and on the second run cleared the
table. For the third game he did the same thing, then
he went on home, feeling more like himself, missing the
entrance to the parking lot and having to back up against
traffic to make it, more than a little surprised when Karen
came running right up to his truck.

Skinny was a little doubtful of the whole situation. Karen
looked genuinely frightened, he gave her that, but he had
the sense about her that she could *look* just about any way
she wanted. She was without doubt sharp enough to have
noted at the party the change in his attitude toward her, and
he had to wonder whether or not she might not now be
trying to get past that by making it appear he was needed.

"I went to set my alarm," she said earnestly, but very
obviously excited, "and the clock wasn't working. So I tried
the lamp. It didn't work, either. He turned off the power to
my apartment."

Skinny glanced at the windows of the other apartments
and saw that many of the lights were still on.

"Who turned off the power?"

"I don't know who he is," Karen replied, "but he's still in

there. He was just getting the sliding glass door open when I made it out through the front door, and he hasn't had time yet to search the whole place."

Karen was standing up on the curb. Skinny was still down on the lot.

"How did he get in through the patio door?"

"He broke the glass," Karen said, her tone edged with impatience. She looked anxiously back toward her apartment, and Skinny glanced at the hem of her T-shirt, which just barely came down to the tops of her thighs.

"Jesus," he said softly, and stepped up onto the sidewalk.

"Well, if you're not going to check it out," Karen said, now obviously disappointed, almost angry, "I guess I should call the police."

"Skinny *is* the police," Skinny said, "but make the call, anyway." He gave her the keys to his apartment so that she could go in to use the phone. "Tell them an officer *may* need assistance."

"The front door is unlocked," Karen offered.

"How handy," Skinny observed.

Karen gave him a sour look that she quickly changed.

"Be careful," she said.

"*That* you can count on," Skinny replied.

He waited for her to walk off and watched as she went up to his door.


At the front door to Karen's apartment, Skinny hesitated only a moment before he went in, long enough to pull his silver gun from his shoulder holster; then he quietly twisted the doorknob until it would turn no further and he was certain that the latch was fully retracted.

He opened the door and went in quickly, just a step, closed the door completely so light would not show behind him. He held the silver revolver pointed down, at the floor, one hand over the other on the rubber Pachmayr grips, feeling very vulnerable as he waited for his eyes to adjust to the very low light in the dark apartment. From the apartment next door, there was the faint sound of a television, but other than that, it was quiet, quiet and still.

Skinny was familiar enough with the complex to know that all the first-floor apartments were laid out the same: the living room was in front of him, the kitchen was to his right, and down the short corridor was the bedroom. When he was able to pick out shapes in the darkness, the big couch just in front of him, low table and chairs beyond it, he inched to his right, sidestepping, keeping his back to the wall. Across from the entrance to the kitchen, he took a deep breath, let it out slowly, stepped across the corridor then swung into the kitchen, swinging the revolver out first, following it around.

The kitchen was empty.

He started to turn back to the corridor, but he saw a shadow move on the counter. He pivoted toward it and felt his grip tighten as the silver gun moved, transcribing a very fast arc, then he saw the gliding shape of Karen's cat, The Butler, the curved line of its back, then its tail, straight up like a flag.

*Close to a dead fucking butler*, he thought, feeling the tension in his neck and shoulders as he relaxed his stance, momentarily allowing the revolver to drop, holding it waist-high.

Glass tinkled lightly in the refrigerator as the cat jumped up on top of it.

Skinny glanced around as he turned, and at the same moment he heard it, he saw it, an intense electric spark moving right toward him, purple-white, a crackling arc of paralyzing electricity an inch and a half long.

He swung the revolver up, toward it, sensing more than seeing the man coming in behind it, and he saw the crackling light glint on the long, silver barrel. Just before the revolver made contact with the zap gun, he realized what he was doing and tried to pull back; then he felt the jolt of high-voltage electricity, like a living thing, running up his right arm past his shoulder, into his neck.

He fell back, hit the stove, kicked out all in one motion, feeling his foot connect solidly with some meaty part of a man. His right arm was at the same time heavy and humming, dangling uselessly at his side. He stepped back, into the corner formed by the stove and the kitchen counter, feeling with his left hand for the revolver in his right. He heard another crackle of electricity, and in that instant he saw the silver revolver in the ghoulish, purple-white light. He saw the sharp creases in his pants and the toes of his polished, black shoes, then he dropped into a vivid, somehow liquid unconsciousness, a blackness much darker than that in Karen's dark apartment.

# 11

He could not understand the voices he heard. While he could hear the words clearly and seemed to understand what they meant, he could give the meanings no sort of context—and without any sense of what had preceded, he had very little sense of what actually was being said. He felt his eyes moving behind his closed lids, moving in an uncomfortable blackness, following the voices, as if on their own. He felt a cool, smooth surface beneath him.

He tried to sit up, lay back, tried again by rolling onto one side and pushing against the floor with his hands. He felt himself lifted under his arms and stood on his feet, placed back into the corner where he had last noticed the shiny black toes on his shoes. When he was able to make his eyes open and then to focus clearly, Skinny saw a paramedic kneeling on the floor, arranging medical supplies in a large fishing-tackle box, then he looked up and saw Karen, Mike Theriot, and the chief of detectives all in the kitchen, all with serious, concerned looks on their faces.

"Jesus Christ," Skinny said. "What a nightmare." He

looked right at Mike Theriot. "Skinny dreamed he was in the same room with the captain."

The captain's name was Ted Grather, and he had been the acting chief of detectives for almost six years, having taken over the job just a few months before Skinny had come up to the bureau. The chief was a fair-minded man, in his own view of himself, fairly patient, and certainly accustomed to verbal abuse.

"The call came out as a signal red," Mike Theriot explained, nervously tapping his long silver flashlight against the side of his leg.

A signal red, Skinny knew, usually meant that shots had been fired at a policeman, and everyone in the vicinity who heard the call rolled, regardless of their rank.

"You phoned that in?" Skinny asked Karen.

"Sort of," Karen replied.

"What happened?" the chief asked.

He glanced at his watch as Skinny glanced at him.

"Skinny has security here," Skinny said. "Free rent—that's particularly helpful when he's not getting a paycheck from the department."

"When he's on suspension, you mean," the chief said calmly, unperturbed.

Mike Theriot grinned, and Skinny saw it.

"Anyway," he went on after he had glared at Mike Theriot, "Skinny was just getting home when he got a report of a burglary in progress."

"From her?" the chief asked, indicating Karen.

"Right," Skinny affirmed. "He came in to check it out and got hit with a zap gun."

The captain seemed to consider that, pursing his lips thoughtfully.

"And that's it?"

"You want more?" Skinny countered, avoiding the question. "Skinny could probably make something up."

The captain was a large man with a big face and closely cut gray hair. When he glanced around the small kitchen, Skinny saw in his gaze the twenty-nine years he had been a policeman. He saw the toughness, the no-nonsense concern, the lack of tolerance for bullshit—and he felt shabby that he had told him only part of the truth.

"Keep me informed," the captain said, then added matter-of-factly, without either malice or humor, "See you next month."

Skinny did not reply to that but watched as he left, for some reason noticing that his own suit was considerably more expensive than the captain's.

"I'm going to pack an overnight bag," Karen said, and went back to her bedroom.

The paramedic closed up his box and left, too.

Skinny watched them both leave, then he turned around, opened a cabinet, found a tall glass, and filled it with water from the tap.

"So how did our burglar cut the power?" he asked Mike Theriot before he drained the glass in one long, overflowing swallow.

"He turned off the switch at the electric meter," Mike Theriot replied as Skinny wiped his chin with the back of his hand. "The meters are numbered." He shrugged. "Nothing to it." He seemed to want to say something else but toyed with his flashlight instead.

Skinny refilled the glass.

"What about the door?"

"What you'd expect."

Mike Theriot waved his flashlight in a way that indicated Skinny should follow, then led the way into the living room.

At the sliding glass door, he pulled the curtains to one side.

"Whoever it was taped the glass, cracked it, then removed the tape and the pieces. She"—he motioned back toward the bedroom—"said she heard the glass break, and that's when she left."

Skinny pretended to study the large, irregular hole in the door-size sheet of glass.

"She ran out the front door, into the parking lot, and saw you coming in. Lucky you." Mike Theriot looked at the door, then looked at Skinny. "Where did you go after you left the party?"

Skinny shook his head, dismissing his whereabouts as unimportant.

"Any witnesses?"

"I've got two uniformed guys checking," Mike Theriot replied, "but I'm not holding my breath." He let the curtains fall back into place. "The crime lab is coming, too. They can try for some prints."

Skinny continued to look right where he had been, as if he could see through the curtains to the sliding door.

"Pull Stan Lee's folder. Get a copy of his picture and take it around to the stores where they sell zap guns."

"You think it was Stan Lee?"

Skinny adjusted his coat as he turned away from the curtains, recalling his impression of Stan Lee when he had first met him, the way his blood had run cold when he had seen his pale, almost colorless eyes and heard the flat, slow twang in his voice.

"What I aim to do," he had said, his first words, "is to start my own fire, the kind we use back home to roast up a beef."

Involuntarily, Skinny glanced back toward Karen's bedroom.

Whoever had broken into the apartment had done so in an

attempt to abduct Karen. That was why they had come in when Karen was home and why they had carried a zap gun—not a pistol or a piece of pipe but a zap gun, a weapon designed to immobilize. While Skinny was not sure that Stan Lee had set either the warehouse fire or the fire in Karen's car, about this he felt reasonably certain.

"I think it was Stan Lee," he said.

"The report came in on the car," Mike Theriot said, as if reading his thoughts. "It was definitely arson. The wires to the instruments had been shorted out in the harness, behind the dash."

Skinny acknowledged that with a nod.

"I'll tell Karen she can get her car back." He loosened his tie then unknotted it, stretching his neck out as he did so, making a face until he was able to get the button loose on his collar. "Have some uniforms pass by the warehouse. If they happen to see Stan Lee, have them hold him for questioning."

"I'll put in a patrol request," Mike Theriot agreed.

"They won't see him," Skinny predicted, patting his pockets, checking to see that nothing would fall out when he took off his coat, realizing only then that his silver revolver was not in his holster. For a moment, he stood noticeably still, then quickly he went back into the kitchen, already knowing that the revolver wasn't there, knowing that the captain or Theriot would have returned it to him if it had been, but checking, anyway, dropping onto all fours to look around on the floor.

Near the baseboard by the dishwasher, there was a fork, but there was nothing else on the floor.

"I already looked," Mike Theriot said behind him. "I saw you didn't have it on you and figured you hadn't come in empty-handed."

Skinny stayed where he was on the floor.

"Is there anything *else* I should know?" he asked, glancing back, seeing Karen, evidently finished her packing, come up next to Mike Theriot.

"Lose your spring again?" she asked very dryly, a disparaging edge on her words.

In one hand she held a small leather suitcase; from the other, a garment bag draped over the side of her shoulder. She had dressed in blue jeans and a starched white cotton shirt.

"No," Skinny replied, stung by her tone, not explaining himself further. Purposely, he took one last look around before he stood up. "Where are you going?"

Karen's blue eyes fixed on his.

"Away from here," she said, her expression hard, close to angry.

"I'll secure the place as much as possible," Mike Theriot offered. When Karen glanced at him, he explained, "I have to wait for the crime lab."

"Whatever," Karen said in a way that made it clear she did not want to be bothered. "I'll send a repairman over tomorrow." She cut her gaze back to Skinny. "You didn't tell me you were on suspension."

"What's suspension?" Skinny replied automatically, forcing the brightness.

Karen, very obviously, was not amused by his answer. The corners of her lips turned down and little lines of irritation appeared on her forehead; yet despite those small signs, there was something about her terse ill humor that was to Skinny not wholly convincing. While he knew that she had lost her car and, in a way, her apartment, still her mood seemed somehow contrived, more, perhaps, what she thought she *should* feel than what she actually did.

"Do you need a ride?" he asked.

"No," she replied. "Thank you. I called a taxi."

She put down the garment bag so that it folded in the middle, then picked it back up by the handle.

"Tonight you can reach me at Morgan Barrett's," she said, addressing herself to Mike Theriot. "Tomorrow I'll be at work."

In order to lift the folded hanging bag high enough that it would not drag on the carpet, Karen had to bend her elbow acutely, obviously straining; and Mike Theriot stepped forward to help her.

"I've got it," she said sharply, refusing his help, and with that she went straight out of the apartment.

Both Skinny and Mike Theriot watched her go, and when the door closed behind her, exchanged glances.

From the parking lot, there was the sound of a car door closing firmly.

"Skinny's going home," Skinny said, "and change clothes."

"I'll call you when the crime lab gets here," Mike Theriot offered.

Skinny glanced around the kitchen one last time and started to leave, but Mike Theriot caught him.

"You look good in a suit," he said. He tapped his flashlight against the side of his leg. "Different."

Skinny stopped in midstride, then started up again, uncertain how to reply.

"Thanks," he said, and went out the same way that Karen had, pulling off his tie and folding it neatly, holding it in one hand, finally making it to his own apartment over an hour after he had turned into the lot.

# 12

Although in his eleven years as a policeman he had many times had justifiable occasion—and twice had even made the attempt—Skinny had never actually shot a man. It wasn't that he had any particular fear or hesitation, it was simply that those two times the right circumstances had presented themselves, when a perpetrator had placed his life in serious danger, Skinny had reacted in his naturally unpredictable fashion, with mixed results. In the first situation, he was already in the process of trying to smack an armed robber on the side of the head with his revolver before he remembered to pull the trigger, an oversight that had left the robber deaf in one ear but not shot; and in the second, he had fired in pitch blackness, aiming, he thought, at the muzzle flashes that were being aimed at him, but no trace of those bullets had ever been found, a ballistic curiosity that had aroused considerable speculation both as to what type of cartridges Skinny had loaded up in the first place and as to where he *had* actually aimed, particularly since the gunfight had taken place in an enclosed parking garage. However, Skinny had both times gotten his man nonetheless, so these two events had not confused *his* thoughts about shooting in any way at all: he knew that if he had to, he would, and if he didn't, he wouldn't—a policy that was so much a part of him he did not even consider it as he took his second-choice service weapon out from under his bed.

Skinny's Colt Series 80 was very different from his revolver. First of all, it had a matte-black finish that did not reflect light. It was .45 caliber, as opposed to .357, semiautomatic, and substantially smaller; and while he felt that the Colt was dynamically superior to the Model 19, particularly in rate of fire, still he liked the silver gun better. He felt more comfortable with it. He felt that he understood it better and that it was more like him. He knew that if he did not get his silver gun back, he'd have to go out and get himself another.

After he had taken the Colt out of its box, prior to cleaning it, he also took out the manual. He read the takedown instructions and followed them carefully, removing the slide release lever as indicated, working the slide as shown in the illustration, chewing his lower lip as all at once the Colt came apart in his hands.

"Now what?" he complained out loud, flipping the pages of the manual back and forth, uncertain what to do with the disassembled pieces.

He decided to clean the pieces before he even thought about reassembly, which was just what he did. But a few minutes later, he was right back where he had been, wondering how the parts fit together, and he decided to go downstairs to get himself a drink.

At the kitchen sink, he filled a tall glass, drank it down, rinsed it out, glancing around as he did so for any other glasses that needed rinsing, too. On the far end of the counter, he saw the half-full glass of champagne just where Karen had left it, and beside it a glass half filled with juice. Looking at those two glasses side-by-side, his first thought was of the waste of pouring yourself more than you would drink, and his second was of Karen, in his apartment after she had called the police, waiting, looking around, a thought that caused in him a slight shift in perspective: he began to try to see his apartment as he supposed Karen had seen it, as if it were new to him, too, as if he were she.

He refilled his water glass and left the half-full glasses right where they were.

In the living room, he noted the patterns in the sofa and the TV tray next to it. He studied the framed picture of his boat, the *No Special Hurry* on its trailer, still wet from Bayou Barataria. He examined the mounted duck in flight on the wall. He was intrigued enough by his effort to see things as Karen had that, when he went back upstairs, he continued to note his various possessions, looking around curiously.

The bathroom was reasonably clean but a mess. Toilet articles were strewn about randomly, out on the counter, within easy reach. There were towels in a heap in one corner. In the bedroom, the closet doors were open revealing a haphazard arrangement of clothes, and the bed was unmade. Most of the toothpaste had oozed back out of the hole he had shot in the wall.

*Figure that*, Skinny thought, amused by the pale blue stalactite of toothpaste, smiling at himself as he wondered what Karen had made of it—and realizing what he had really known all along, that no matter how hard he tried, he would never quite see things as she did. He glanced out the window at the pool, briefly picturing her as he had first seen her, all greased up for the sun, then he looked at the pieces of his pistol, laid out neatly where he had put them, on the end of the bed.

"Jesus Christ," he said softly, his eyes narrowing, fixed on the Colt's big recoil spring, now *really* thinking of Karen, suddenly remembering when in the parking lot he had first noticed her fist and figured out that she had his rebound slide spring.

"Jesus Christ," he said again.

Just as when he had seen Karen's fist, Skinny had known that she had the spring, now he was certain that she had his revolver. It made perfect sense.

Skinny stepped over to the window and looked out, confirming what he already knew: from his window, Karen's patio door was clearly visible—as easy to see as the likely sequence.

Karen had seen whoever it was leave, and she had gone back to her apartment. She had seen Skinny, unconscious, and she had seen the silver gun, both on the floor. She had hidden the gun and gone back outside to wait for the police, then she had taken the gun with her when she left, deciding her mood in advance, playing it just right, not even letting Theriot help with her suitcase, afraid that he might feel the weight.

*She has Skinny's silver gun*, Skinny thought, picturing Karen unpacking it, hiding it again in Morgan Barrett's house, *and she's already used it against him.*

Skinny shook his head side to side, disturbed that it had taken him so long to see it.

The curtains opened behind Karen's patio door, and a crime lab technician appeared, examining the hole in the glass.

For a brief moment, Skinny wondered whether or not

Karen wanted the revolver for any purpose other than to distract him, but the technician saw him and waved, signaling him to come down, distracting him again, so he did not answer his own question—which, if he had thought about it at all, he would have figured out right away.

# 13

After leaving Skinny and Mike Theriot exchanging glances, befuddled by her unexpected display of anger, Karen got into the taxi she had called from her bedroom, ordered the driver just to drive off, then told him to stop at the first pay phone he saw.

The driver complied without comment and stopped at a pay phone near the entrance to a nearby motel.

Karen tried to reach Morgan both at home and at his office, but neither call was answered; so she decided to go on to the warehouse district where she could wait in her office until she could reach Morgan to tell him that she was about to be a guest at his house.

When the taxi pulled up to Grover's building, Karen was annoyed to see that the office lights were still on. Not wanting anyone to see her carrying her bags, particularly not the janitors who, she assumed, were there late to clean up after the party, she told the taxi driver to wait while she went on inside.

But the office was already clean. The folding buffet tables had been removed, and the office furniture had been returned to its normal arrangement. The carpet had been vacuumed and showed no sign of the guests who had been there just a few hours before. From the back, however, behind the open area where the secretaries sat, she heard conversation, and she went down the aisle between the secretaries' desks, stopping to listen at the doorway that led to the offices beyond. When she recognized Grover's voice, she went on, curious to find Grover and Morgan in one of the conference rooms, already reviewing the list of guests who had been invited to the party. Grover was sitting at a glass-topped table, his back to the door, a computer printout open in front of him, and Morgan was stretched out on the couch, his head propped up on the armrest.

Grover said, "Her dog got sick, that's why she wasn't here. She had to rush it to a clinic in England."

"She took her dog to England?" Morgan asked, not looking away from the ceiling, his tone very dry.

"England," Grover affirmed. "Can you believe it? It's an English sheepdog and she says she just knows it gets homesick—she called from the airport to tell me. She's crazy as a loon, but she has *so* much money she gets away with it. The old bag. I hate her."

"But Grover," Karen said, choosing that moment to reveal her presence, knowing exactly whom he was talking about, "I thought she was one of your *dearest* friends."

"Well of course she is," Grover replied, not bothering to look back—and not missing a beat. "Don't I stay in her apartment every time I go to New York?"

"Grover," Karen said disparagingly, walking all the way into the room, "you're such a shit."

Grover laughed pleasantly at that, amused.

Karen stood by the table and turned the printout so that she could see it.

"This is *my* printout," she observed, her emphasis conveying her displeasure. "These are my notes in the margins."

"I couldn't find mine," Grover replied lightly, "and you're just so organized—there your copy was, right on your desk." Grover turned on his chair and casually rested his elbow on the back of it. "I love your notes, too," he added, waving his hand at the printout. "Who was that you wrote about?" His quick eyes darted to Morgan. "Old family. Old money. Old bitch."

Karen picked up the printout and pointedly tucked it under her arm.

"Old family. Old money. Old bitch," Morgan repeated, as if getting it straight. "How clever." He rolled his head on the armrest just enough to glance at Karen. "But if you ask me, judging from this evening's response to your little show—or should I say, the evening's lack of response—you should be searching out *new* money." He looked back at the ceiling. "Old money gets to be old because somebody keeps a tight rein on it." His slightly bored tone took on a suggestive authority. "Hustle up a few more doctors. Find a car dealer or two. Your sales aren't exactly booming."

Karen knew immediately what Morgan was really saying, and why; and she felt an angry flush rise to her cheeks, as if she had been slapped.

"Bullshit," she said, choosing just then to reply only to the words he had actually said. "The sales are doing well enough."

Morgan lazily turned his head and looked at Karen again, his thin lips pulled back slightly, as close to a smile as he ever came.

"If you say so," he said.

"I say so," Karen affirmed, her bright blue eyes hard as glass.

"This is so much fun," Grover remarked.

"Grover," Karen said, not concerned about Grover at all, even pleased that he had said something distracting. "Take a hike." When she glanced at him, Grover winked, as if to give her encouragement and to show that they were on the same side. "Take two hikes," she said, knowing better, having seen him use that same wink on a property owner just before he bought his property for a fraction of its real worth. She turned back to Morgan. "I'm going to stay at your house," she reported.

Morgan looked over, mildly curious.

"Will *that* be enough to improve sales?" Grover asked.

Karen did not acknowledge that in any way at all. For years, she had spent the night at the Barrett house whenever she wanted. Morgan's father had liked her—he had even given her a key—and he had invited her to stay whenever she pleased, which she had, after parties or when she was out late or whenever she hadn't felt like going to her father's and dealing with whatever ex-wife he had home at the moment. There was certainly room enough for her in the huge house.

"Somebody broke into my apartment this evening," she went on matter-of-factly. "There's no way to lock my door."

Morgan seemed to weigh that information very carefully.

"It's not exactly your week, is it?" he observed. "I'm glad I'm not your insurer." He sat up on the couch by rolling onto one shoulder and pushing himself up with his hands. "Did they steal anything?"

"No," Karen replied. "The security guard ran them off." Morgan stared at his shoes.

"What a nuisance," he remarked, then he added, "Not for me, of course. For you." He stood up and buttoned his suit coat. "I was about to leave. I'll give you a ride." Absently, he patted his pockets, not really searching for anything, just checking that he was in order. "It just occurred to me," he said, glancing at Grover, then back at Karen, his hands suddenly still. "With your car out of commission, a car dealer might be handy for you two ways." He showed his amused hint of a smile.

Karen felt the anger again, the flush in her cheeks.

"Keep it up," she replied, holding up her fist and shaking it at Morgan, appearing to take his comment as a joke. "Keep it up and you'll be searching out a few doctors for yourself."

"Fight! Fight!" Grover said, laughing lightheartedly but pleased to be sitting off to the side.

# 14

Skinny had stayed up late. He had waited for the uniformed officers to complete the canvass of the complex and he had waited for the crime lab technician to complete his tests. As he waited, he had poked around in Karen's apartment, and an hour later, when neither the canvass nor the tests turned up anything helpful, he had gone home and reassembled the Colt. And after he had gone to bed, the Colt back in working order, not surprisingly he had found that he was too wound up to sleep. So he had gone back downstairs and watched old movies on television until finally he had dozed off for a few hours on the couch, then he had gotten up early and gone right back out, getting to the warehouse district just before seven o'clock. He found the parking lot behind Grover's building that was reserved for employees and parked across the street from it, sipping a cup of coffee he had picked up from the Hummingbird Grill, waiting for Ruth.

Ruth arrived early. She pulled up a few minutes after seven-thirty, stopped at the entrance to the lot, and got out of her compact car to unlock the big chain link gate. She pushed the gate open, rolling it sideways along its track, and when it was just wide enough open, Skinny slipped into the lot, going right past her and parking in a space marked RESERVED.

When Ruth pulled into the lot, Skinny was already out of his truck, standing beside it, smiling brightly.

Ruth parked three spaces down, opened the door of her car, and said, "It may be a little too early for you," before she even got out.

"It's never too early for Skinny," Skinny said, going up to her, taking his overlong strides, watching as she reached to the passenger seat and picked up her briefcase, transferred it to her left hand, then reached back and picked up the brown paper bag that held her lunch.

"How about some breakfast?" he asked.

Ruth turned sideways on the car seat to look up at him. She put her briefcase on her lap and her lunch on top of it.

"I can't," she replied.

"Sure you can," Skinny went right back at her. "You go inside and turn on the lights. Put some papers on your desk. Make it look like you got here real early and went back out—Skinny does it all the time." Skinny smiled as if he had thought of something truly clever. "He gets to work right before shift change."

Ruth smiled indulgently. The low yellow sunlight clearly showed her makeup and the unflattering, grainy texture in it; but it also showed the clarity in her hazel eyes, the red-brown in the green, and her good humor.

"Ruth gets to choose the place?" she asked.

"Skinny was thinking of the Hummingbird," Skinny replied.

"Ruth suspected Skinny was thinking of the Hummingbird —that's why she asked if she got to choose the place."

Skinny looked right at her, acting a little put out.

"Ruth gets to choose the place," he conceded.

Ruth smiled again and stood up.

"I'll just go scatter some papers," she said, holding her lunch and her briefcase in one hand, closing the car door with the other.

"Skinny'll just wait," Skinny said.

Ruth did not reply to that but looked through the keys on her oversize brass key ring, picking out the right one.

The back door to Grover's building was gray steel, and Skinny watched as Ruth unlocked it and went inside, then he leaned back against the side of her car. After a minute of leaning, he opened the door and sat down where Ruth had, on the edge of the driver's seat. When the steering wheel touched his back, he twisted around, pretending that the touch had disturbed him, giving himself an excuse to examine the car.

The interior smelled of cigarette smoke, and behind that there was the flat, musty smell of incipient mold. The brown vinyl dashboard was sun-faded and, in one place near the middle, starting to crack. On the passenger-side seat, there was an open box of tissues, and on the passenger-side floor, there was enough paper—receipts, underwiper ads, the sports section from an old newspaper, even a partially flattened shoe box—to fill up a medium-size trash can. In his mind's eye, Skinny started to compare Ruth's car to Karen's, before the fire, of course, but he dug out the old newspaper instead and read the baseball statistics, surprised when Ruth suddenly reappeared.

"I thought you needed a warrant to search a car," she said, dryly announcing her presence.

"To search your car," Skinny replied, not looking up from the American League standings, "what you'd need is a scoop shovel." He closed the paper and tossed it back where he had found it on the floor. "Skinny's just naturally curious," he added as he stood up. "So where are we going for breakfast?"

Ruth ignored Skinny's question and went over to his truck and looked in the window.

"Oh, my," she said, looking back.

"Jesus Christ," Skinny protested, and closed the door to Ruth's car. "It's not like we're giving inspections."

Ruth smiled, obviously gratified by the mess she had seen in the truck.

"There's a cafe on the corner," she said, foreshortening her smile to a grin.

Skinny allowed her to start out of the lot, then went up beside her.

"Why are you here so early?" he asked.

"In case you've forgotten," Ruth replied, "I work here." Although she smiled when she said it, there was the resigned wage earner sound to her tone that added without saying the words *I have to be here.* "I like to be the first to the office," she went on. "It's quiet. It gives me a few minutes to plan my day."

Ruth was wearing a sleeveless white blouse and a long, very loose green skirt. She put her hand in the pocket of the skirt, left it there briefly, then took it out again, glancing at Skinny as she did so, the obvious question a curious look in her eyes.

"Skinny's working a case," Skinny explained. "That's why he's here."

"The fire in the warehouse?"

"Right. The warehouse that Grover just bought."

Skinny started to say something else, but Ruth looked to one side in a way that made Skinny's gaze follow her gaze, through the big plate glass front of a bakery-cafe.

"This is it?" he asked.

Ruth nodded in reply and bent forward, her face near the glass as she studied the pastries displayed.

"Oh, my," she said again.

Skinny did not look at the pastries at all but looked at her, amused and somehow pleased by the ready pleasure she took in the ridiculously sumptuous display.

"I'll make it easy," Ruth said, standing up straight. "I'll have one of each."

Inside, they both ordered lemon Danish pastries and coffee, then they sat at a small, porcelain-topped table that tipped whenever one or the other of them touched it. Ruth ate around the center of her Danish, saving the lemon filling for last, while Skinny started in on one side of his and went right on through to the other. Ruth looked out the big window as she nibbled and chewed, blankly watching the street.

Skinny said, "Skinny's not a big believer in coincidence." After his last bite of pastry, he licked the tips of his fingers and wiped them on the legs of his jeans. "He thinks it's overrated as an explanation."

Ruth handed him a paper napkin from the dispenser, then took one for herself.

"What does coincidence have to do with the fire?" she asked, sensing his direction, and curious, but still preoccupied with her Danish.

"The fire wasn't coincidence at all," Skinny replied. "The fire was arson."

He tipped the table his way when he put his elbows on it and roughly wiped his mouth with the napkin.

"Grover made three offers to buy the building, and all

three offers were refused. Then it gets torched and guess what? The business is out of operation, and the owner doesn't want it anymore. He sells it to Grover the day after the fire—just in time for his party."

Ruth dabbed at her lips with the paper napkin she had taken for herself, trying to remove the flakes of sugar at the corners of her mouth without smearing her lipstick.

"Maybe the owner set the fire himself. Or maybe a competitor saw the opportunity—"

"Maybe a lot of things," Skinny interrupted her. "But that's not the point. The point is, what you have here is a big, fat coincidence."

Ruth looked at her napkin, then crumpled it around the red smears her lipstick had left.

"And Skinny's not a big believer in coincidence."

"Right," Skinny affirmed. He sat back, and the table tipped. He caught it and held it with his hands. "The only *real* coincidence Skinny's ever heard of is the alignment of the planets—and he's not even sure he's convinced about that."

Ruth grinned wanly, her expression unformed but thoughtful. Either her attention was still on her pastry or she was beginning to discern what he was leading up to; but her eyes were off somewhere else, too vague for Skinny to tell which.

"I think I'll have some milk," she said suddenly, and moved her chair away from the table to stand up.

For a fraction of a second, Skinny caught her gaze, and it took him a few moments to realize how wrong he had just been. Her eyes weren't vague at all; they were troubled. She wasn't behind him, only beginning to discern his direction, she was *ahead* of him, already bothered by something. And if that was the case, likely that something was disturbing her as much as a loose tooth she could not leave alone as she tried to resolve where her loyalty to her employer ended—which, Skinny knew, for someone like Ruth could be a very tough nut to crack.

Skinny sat forward again, his own expression unformed, as he tried to decide how to help Ruth resolve her dilemma.

Ruth sat down tentatively, on the edge of her chair, sipped the glass of milk she had just bought, put the glass down, and glanced at her wristwatch.

"I have to go," she said. "I'll be late."

Skinny's eyes were level on hers.

"A man died in the fire," he said.

Ruth's eyes flicked away.

"I know," she replied.

Skinny was certain then that he had not misread her the second time because the troubled look was back on her face; but now there was pain, too, pain and confusion.

She stood up, started to say something, stopped herself.

After a moment, Skinny asked, "Are you through with your milk?"

Ruth nodded.

Skinny picked up the almost-full glass and drained it in one long, uninterrupted swallow.

"Skinny likes milk," Skinny said, smiling in a self-satisfied way, like a boy who had just performed a neat trick for his friends, "but he always forgets to get it."

Ruth grinned uncertainly, then left, going out the door and past the cafe's big plate glass windows, glancing again at her watch.

Skinny sat very still, only his eyes following her until she passed out of sight. When he shortened his gaze and sat back, away from the table, looping his arm over the back of the chair, he absently noted the piece of Danish Ruth had left before he stood up and cleaned off the table.

# 15

Skinny had decided that Morgan Barrett was much more interesting than Grover. For one thing, according to Ruth he had more money; and for another, he had known Karen substantially longer. So from the bakery-cafe Skinny found a phone booth and looked up Morgan's address, found the street on the map he kept in his truck, then headed out to Morgan's house, knowing even as he did it that he was, very likely, just giving himself reasons to go see what he was curious about anyway.

On the expressway, the morning traffic going into town was bumper-to-bumper, but the outbound traffic was light. Skinny watched the incoming cars crawling along as he drove past them at high speed, feeling smug that he was headed in the opposite direction, wondering how all those people summoned up all that patience before they even began their workday.

From the expressway, Skinny turned off onto a highway, and after a short distance he turned off that, going about a mile down a very straight street with small, modest houses on either side. He crossed a broad, open canal, and at the same time crossed into the next parish. A few hundred yards later, the street turned, and Skinny slowed down, knowing instinctively that Morgan's house was not far away.

The street had become considerably wider in the turn, allowing room for a broad median that was landscaped with flowers and neatly trimmed plants. Live oaks had been planted on the median and on both sides of the street, and their huge branches met overhead, over the street, forming a green canopy, almost a tunnel a quarter mile long. Set well back from the street, the houses were spaced far apart. Other streets led off this central one, and Skinny checked his map to see which way he should turn, going slowly, glancing at the map then at the big houses.

Morgan Barrett's house was on a corner. In front, a broad, brick walkway led up to the door. On either side of the door, there were two large, highly polished brass lanterns, shining brightly, gas flames flickering within. The house itself was red brick trimmed out with white, and it was huge, almost as big as an entire wing of Skinny's apartment complex. Behind the house, only the top of it visible behind a high brick wall, there was some sort of pavilion, bright yellow and white canvas stretched over a frame. There were plants and trees everywhere, banana trees and oak trees, shrubs, flowers, and, in the backyard, even a palm tree. The front yard was big enough for field hockey.

Skinny drove down the street that ran beside Morgan's house, turned around and drove back up it. He parked where he could see both the front and the side of the house and turned off the engine, settling in for a wait, pleased that he was in his truck, knowing that he was inconspicuous among the various service vehicles that were already coming and going, the gardeners, painters, and swimming pool maintenance men there early to fine-tune the big houses and to keep them pristine.

Skinny was surprisingly patient about surveillance. Although he had never liked it, he recognized the need for it and as a result had worked hard to attain the necessary patience. He had learned to sit very still for hours, only his eyes moving, noting—and even taking some pleasure in—the small events that became apparent after watching the same scene for some length of time. While watching Morgan Barrett's house, he saw how the affluent neighborhood came quietly to life, in many ways beginning the day not all that much differently from his old neighborhood in Gentilly. He saw the husbands and wives leaving separately—usually the man left first, in a sedan, his expression intent and purposeful; and the woman came out sometime later, in a station wagon or even larger sedan, not quite as single-minded as her husband had been, trying to remember all the things that she had to do. He saw the perfunctory good-byes, the trips back inside for items forgotten, the young children hurried into cars or teenagers taking off in cars of their own. As the sun got higher, in the big oak trees he noticed the squirrels scrambling about in the branches, one or two brazenly crossing the big lawns, running in spurts, pausing to look about, their dark eyes wary but not really afraid. It all seemed very orderly, orderly and peaceful and quiet. Later on, he saw the arrival of the maids in their white uniforms, a few driving but most walking, moving deliberately, their eyes fixed straight ahead, on some point only they could see.

An old car stopped in front of Morgan's house, and an old black woman got out. She went up the front walkway as the car drove off, rang the doorbell, then let herself into the house with a key. A few minutes later, the big gates in the wall along the side of the house began to swing out, opening electrically.

Skinny started his truck and allowed the engine to idle.

Until they were all the way open, the black iron gates obscured what was behind them; but once open, from his position down the block Skinny could see almost all of the driveway.

Karen and Morgan were standing between cars, beneath the flat roof of the four-car carport, waiting for the gates to stop moving. Morgan was dressed in a dark suit and was carrying a briefcase. Karen wore white slacks and a tan blouse. As soon as the gates stopped, Morgan opened the driver's door on a shiny black Mercedes, tossed in the briefcase, then got in himself. He said something to Karen through the window, which was, apparently, already open, started the car, and immediately put it in reverse. As Morgan backed the Mercedes out of the driveway, Karen went around the front of a midsize gray Ford and got into that car. There was some delay while she adjusted the seat and found the car's controls, but in short order she was following Morgan, backing behind him, out of the driveway.

"It must be handy," Skinny said to himself, watching the small movements with interest, deciding right then to follow Karen if she went a different direction than Morgan, "to have a spare *car*."

Morgan pulled far enough down the street to allow Karen to get out of the driveway, then activated the remote control for the gates. When the gates began to move again, he drove to the corner, rolled through the stop sign, and set out for wherever it was he was going, Karen right on his bumper.

Skinny put his truck in gear but stayed right where he was, knowing that Karen would recognize the truck if he followed too closely—and knowing, too, that he could easily catch up to her on the long, straight street that was the only way out of the area.

Just as the car Karen was driving went out of sight, an old Chevrolet turned down the same street.

"Damn," Skinny said, starting out hurriedly, jerking his truck up to speed, wanting to get in front of the car as quickly as possible; but for two blocks, he could not even catch up.

"Hot damn," he said, two blocks after that beginning to realize that whoever was in the car was following Karen, too, taking the same turns, driving with purpose, trying to keep her in sight.

Skinny did not notice the big houses now. He was concentrating on his driving, allowing the Chevrolet a good lead on the straights and catching up on the turns; and driving like that, his attention diverted, it was not until he was on the long, straight street with the live oaks overhead that he noticed the car behind *him*.

"Jesus Christ," he said out loud, checking the rearview mirror again, more than a little perturbed. "What is this? A fucking parade?"

Sunlight and shadow washed over the windshield of the canary-yellow Cadillac behind him, and Skinny could not see who was driving. He glanced forward then back, trying to keep track of both cars at once, making his decision as the tree-lined street ended and he reached the canal.

Just past the turn in the road, without warning he put the wheel of the truck over hard, sliding it sideways across both lanes of traffic, and before it had stopped moving he jumped out, grabbing the tire iron he kept under his seat for just such occasions, too excited to really register the fact that the Cadillac was skidding right toward him.

The Cadillac came to a stop less than ten feet away, and

when Skinny saw who was driving, he unhesitatingly stepped up and swung the tire iron, using both hands, swinging it like a very short bat.

The driver's window exploded.

Skinny threw down the tire iron, reached into the car, grabbed the front of a shirt and a handful of hair, and dragged Stan Lee out through the window, bumping him roughly over the sill, rudely dropping him as soon as he was most of the way out.

Stan Lee rolled onto his back to untangle his legs, dazed, pushing himself up on his elbows, obviously surprised to find himself out on the street.

Skinny started to say something to him but picked up his tire iron instead and went to the back of the car. Using the wedge-shaped end of the heavy metal bar, he bent the trunk lid out, bending the metal until the lock popped; then he searched the trunk, throwing old clothes, empty beer cans, and hand tools out behind him, looking as if he were burrowing.

"Where is it?" he asked Stan Lee as he stepped over him, finished his search of the trunk, and went around and opened the door.

"Where is what?" Stan Lee asked in reply, quickly sliding back out of the way. "That's an illegal search," he added petulantly, "and you know it."

Skinny sat on the driver's seat, leaned over and went through the glove box, then felt along under the seats. When he found what he had been looking for, he got back out of the car.

He held the zap gun up close to his face, examining it curiously.

"You get hit with this thing," he said, shifting his attention to Stan Lee, squeezing the trigger that activated the zap gun, punctuating his comment with a purple-white arc of crackling electricity, "it hurts like shit."

Stan Lee just looked back at him, his pale, clear eyes hooded, assessing and wary, but unafraid.

"It feels like needles."

"It don't feel too good," Stan Lee observed, "getting yanked out the window of your car."

Skinny looked again at the zap gun, then put it away, in his hip pocket, shrugging to himself and for the moment calling them even.

"So, Stan Lee," he said, starting off in a new direction, "you've been busy since Skinny last saw you." Skinny leaned back against the inside of the open car door and crossed his ankles. He picked up several pieces of broken safety glass from the top of the door and shook them in one hand. "You sold your building. You broke into Karen's apartment—"

"I don't know nothing about that," Stan Lee interrupted him.

"And now," Skinny went on as if he hadn't heard him, "here you are, following Skinny." Skinny stopped rattling the pebbles of glass. "Stan Lee, just what are you up to?"

Stan Lee seemed to enjoy Skinny's question because he smiled thinly, in an amused, secretive way.

"I did sell my building," he admitted finally. "I got a good price for it, too, everything considered." He pushed himself up to a sitting position, then got to his feet, dusting off the seat of his pants. "I don't know nothing—"

"About Karen's apartment," Skinny finished for him. "Skinny heard you the first time." He shook the pieces of glass again, then threw them away, glancing at the open canal as he did so, seeing the steep banks lined with concrete and in the distance one of the huge pumps that drained the city when it rained. "So are you following Skinny, or what?" he asked, looking back at Stan Lee.

Stan Lee had bought himself a new yellow sport shirt as bright as the one he had been wearing when Skinny had first met him. He reached into the shirt's pocket, took out a pack of unfiltered cigarettes, removed one, and returned the pack to the pocket.

"The way I figure it," he replied, "a man has to be sure he's gettin' the value out of his money." Cupping his big hands around the flame, he lit the cigarette with a lighter. He took a deep pull, then exhaled through his nose. "When a man is buying a service, he's obliged to keep an eye on how things are progressin'."

"What's that supposed to mean?" Skinny asked sourly, catching his drift and not sure that he liked it. "You posted a reward. That's not what you call buying a service."

"It's the same thing to me," Stan Lee disagreed, ducking his head and smiling apologetically. "I'm spending my money to get what I want." He held the cigarette at the very tips of two yellow-stained fingers. "You seem to be doin' okay."

Skinny did not dignify that with a comment.

"You just stick after the girl," Stan Lee advised. "She'll lead you to the man killed my partner."

"Unless you get to her first, right?" Skinny interjected.

Stan Lee smiled his amused smile again.

"Skinny'd hate for anything to happen to the girl, Stan Lee," Skinny said calmly. "He'd have to think that you did it. Then Skinny'd have to come after you."

Stan Lee rubbed his chin with the back of the hand in which he was holding his cigarette. He looked off, down the canal.

"If you say so," he said.

"Skinny says so," Skinny affirmed.

After a few moments, Stan Lee took a final pull on his cigarette, then twisted around and flipped it back, over his car and over the bridge railing, into the canal. Without a word, he went to the back of his car and retrieved the clothes and tools Skinny had thrown out on the ground—he left the empty beer cans right where they were. That done, he moved past Skinny and brushed the broken glass from the seat of his car, got in, and waited patiently—smiling agreeably, looking off in the distance—for Skinny to move his truck.

Skinny looked at him until he got tired of looking, not saying anything, knowing there was no way to reason with Stan Lee this side of his Louisville Slugger.

# 16

Although he had not known who he was—and had been thrown off at first by the truck, not expecting a pickup to be used for surveillance—Rick Trask had seen Skinny behind him and had known instinctively that he was the police.

Rick had been surprised at how calmly that fact had registered, how matter-of-factly he had dealt with it. He had continued to follow Karen, going fast enough to run right up behind her, seeing her startled expression when she recognized him in her rearview mirror; then just before the canal, he had turned off, slipping down the one-way street that ran beside the canal, turning again as soon as he could, cutting in and out of a labyrinth of streets until he was satisfied that the pickup could not possibly still be behind him.

On a quiet street, he pulled to the curb and turned off his car, feeling his hands shaking slightly and a quivering sensation in his chest—feeling at the same time both pleased with himself and angry, knowing how lucky he had been.

He unwrapped a mint, put it in his mouth, and sucked on it, hard, savoring the taste.

He put his head back on the headrest.

Rick wanted Karen to know he was after her. He wanted her afraid. He wanted her to feel helpless, panicked, alone— since he had set fire to the warehouse, he had felt all those things. And more. He had felt an anger he found hard to restrain, there all the time, just beneath the surface.

For the thirteen years he had been a fireman, he had been all right. He had been a little cocky, he knew, and at times a lot selfish, but he had done his job and had never backed down from it. No one could say differently. He had stood up close to the fires and gone into them when he had had to—and he had been burned twice, badly, for his trouble. He had stood the long, boring watches, polished the trucks and equipment, sat in on the requisite marathon games of poker. He had done everything by the numbers, just like you were supposed to. He had paid his union dues, the note on the house that was no longer his, the note on his car. Regular as clockwork. And look what he had to show for it.

Rick sucked the mint so hard the candy's rough edges cut into the roof of his mouth.

He had an ex-wife who sent him notes through an attorney, a bleak, three-room apartment in a marginal neighborhood, a car in need of its third set of tires.

*Who could blame me*, he thought, *for trying to make extra money?*

But he already knew the answer to that: any jury that heard the facts would convict him. And rightfully so. He was guilty.

*He was guilty*.

With one hand, Rick rubbed the back of his neck, feeling the knots in the muscles. He rotated his head as he pressed his fingers in hard, trying to relax, trying not to think, finding that, for no apparent reason, his glance kept moving back to the empty seat next to him. It took him several moments to realize what had caught his attention, a half-formed image of Karen when she had sat there, on the seat, turned toward him, leaning forward, that hungry look in her eyes after she had watched a fire; and for several minutes he allowed the reverie to develop, making no effort to stop it. He allowed himself to replay when he had met her, reviewing the scene in detail, seeing it and seeing what had followed until it was so real to him he could smell her. He could feel the heat she gave off.

He put the mint between his back teeth and cracked it, unaware of even the sound.

He had been in the moving company's office, he recalled, behind the desk when she had come in and announced, "I'm moving. And I *like* fires."

"What you should do, Miss—?" he had said.

"Karen," she had filled in the blank. "Karen Hodges."

"Karen Hodges," he had repeated. "You should pile all your furniture on your bed. Douse it with some gasoline. And burn it—have a nice little fire and save all the expense of moving."

He had expected her to be surprised by that, thrown off, but she had surprised him instead, actually seeming to consider the suggestion, her bright blue eyes going blank for a moment, thoughtful, as if she were in her mind already stacking the furniture.

*That was a new one*, Rick thought, giving her credit. *I should have known then.*

But he had just sat back and looked at her dully, concealing his interest, tapping the pencil he held against the back of his thumb. When the UHF radio had sounded, he had watched her watching it, listening to the call, allowing his eyes to wander over her, lingering on the front of her shirt. And when he had suggested that they go to see the fire the dispatcher had just reported, she had not hesitated for a second.

"We went in the truck," Rick said out loud, as if to another person, laughing at himself, at his own transparent intentions.

At the fire, he had stood in the street.

Karen had stood up on the curb next to him, her eyes shining as she had watched the three-story wood-frame building burning out of control. The day had been sunny and clear. The heat had been a presence, a dry, searing pressure. The flames had made a constant, rushing roar. Ten minutes into it, the roof of the building had collapsed, throwing fiery embers, and he had put his arm around her waist. More than the heat, he had felt the swell of her hips and the slick glide of her slacks as he had moved his hand, dropping it down, moving it in slow circles.

She had leaned against him, pressing her breast against his ribs.

A fireman Rick knew had seen him and nodded in his direction.

Rick had smiled in reply, and dropped his hand lower. He had moved his hand across her hips, feeling that glide and swell, then slipped it up, between her legs. He had heard her gasp, a sharp intake of breath, but she had not looked away from the fire.

Before the third alarm had gone out, calling for another company, he had moved her to the back of the truck.

It had been hot in there, he remembered, hot and dark, musty with the smell of the quilted green packing blankets. He had not kissed her but had unbuttoned her blouse, then quickly pulled off his shirt. He had plunged his arm between her legs and lifted her, pressing the inside of his forearm against her mound, and put her across the pile of blankets, her back arched over them. In one motion he had pulled off her slacks and panties, then he had taken off his own pants; and that quickly he had fallen down onto her and into her full-length, feeling powerful lying over her, bigger in every way, at least a hundred pounds heavier, his weight alone pinning her down.

Without realizing that he was doing so, Rick shifted on the seat of his car and glanced around the quiet neighborhood where he was parked, as if someone watching could see him pounding Karen, throwing himself at her, over and over, as if they could hear the wet, slapping sound of their bellies. With startling clarity, suddenly he remembered that in the back of the truck for a few minutes his eyes had been closed. He remembered when he had opened them again because at that moment he understood what he had seen, more than the image itself, an understanding that made both a deep, hollow sadness and an anger near rage surge through him: he had seen Karen watching him, her eyes narrowed, the gleam behind her lashes hard and silvery as light on a cold, pointed blade, calculating. He saw that all the time they had spent together, the nights in his apartment, Karen curled up next to him, her fingers tracing the ugly white-brown ridges of his scars, touching them gently as if mapping them in her mind, the afternoons they had just sat around, listening to the UHF radio, watching each other, waiting for a good fire and knowing what would come after, the tension palpable between them, the time she had invited him out, to a play, making him feel comfortable and special, the breakfasts and showers together and the late night phone calls that had always begun, "Do you know what I'm doing right now?" all that had been contrived from the start, part of a calculated plan that had left him right where he was, in a world of shit and knowing that she had planned it that way, certain that he would be unable to do anything about it, certain of the power she had over him because *she* was the only one who could make him as an arsonist.

"Goddammit," Rick said, and angrily slammed his fist against the dashboard, the knowledge of what he had to do—what she was *forcing* him to do—coming immediately to mind, putting a hard edge on the anger, an edge that a few moments later cut down to a deep, overwhelming despair.

"No!" Rick bellowed in the closed car, a sound like that he had made when he had seen the man in the warehouse engulfed in flames, yellow fire suddenly dancing the length of him. "No!"

# 17

Ruth said, "I was always too tall. I was a girl, of course, and still I was always the tallest person in my class. And I was *skinny*. Skinny and gangly—Skinny doesn't know what it *means* to be skinny, not next to Ruth."

"Skinny has a pretty good idea," Skinny said.

They were sitting in a booth in a restaurant that served Mexican food. Over their heads was a stained-glass lamp that hung on a chain from the ceiling. On the table between them was a basket of chips that supplemented those that had come with the guacamole. When Skinny had checked in at the office, Mike Theriot had told him that Ruth had called, so he had called her and they had agreed to meet for lunch. Skinny had ordered the chips and the guacamole. Ruth was content with the margaritas: she had drunk the first one down fast and was already well into a second.

"In gym class," Ruth went on, "I was always the last one chosen for the teams."

"Not because you were skinny," Skinny said with certainty.

Ruth shook her head as she took another swallow from her drink.

"Because I was a klutz," she laughed. She put the drink down on the table but kept her hand wrapped around it. "I was growing too fast, and besides that I was as blind as a bat."

Ruth paused long enough to light one of her long, thin cigarettes. She took a puff, then held the cigarette beside her leg, out of sight.

"When I was five, my mother took me to get glasses. I didn't like them at all—"

"Why not?" Skinny asked.

"Because then I could *see*," Ruth replied, smiling readily but not really answering the question. "Anyway," she continued, "my mother let me pick out the frames for the glasses myself, but I couldn't see what they looked like until the lenses had been put in them. So I wound up with these cat's-eye frames studded with rhinestones. God, they were ugly. They made me look like a bean pole wearing oversize reflectors—if I had been my mother, I would have traded me in."

Skinny smiled at that as he took a chip and crunched it. He knew exactly what Ruth was doing, how she was digressing, avoiding what was really on her mind until she worked up the courage to tell him, and he didn't mind a bit. He liked Ruth. He liked her straightforward way of thinking and her candor. He even liked her sense of humor, and he knew she would get to her point soon enough.

"You don't wear glasses now," he observed.

"I had an operation," Ruth confided, looking off in a way that indicated she did not wish to pursue the specifics.

She took another puff from her cigarette and Skinny took another chip.

"When the oil industry went bad a few years ago," Ruth started up again, looking back, "my parents had to leave New Orleans—my father was laid off and couldn't find work."

There was sadness in her tone, sadness with a trace of bitterness.

"What's your father do?" Skinny asked.

"He's an electrician," Ruth replied. "He worked the rigs, offshore—he went to Houston thinking he could find work there and ended up having to take a job as a short-order cook."

Ruth flicked ashes into the ashtray she had set on the bench beside her leg. Her face turned away, in profile Skinny could see the strain she felt, the strain and the incomprehension.

"He thought he could do his job well and be dependable and honest and that would be enough. But that's not enough, is it?"

"It takes a little luck, too," Skinny said.

Ruth's lips moved slightly, turning up; but her overstressed expression made the gesture more a tick than a smile.

"My father is a carpenter," Skinny offered.

Ruth continued to look down a few moments longer, then she looked up and smiled, pushing back the emotion she had just felt.

"It's the tequila," she said, and put her margarita on Skinny's side of the table, out of easy reach. "I don't know why I drink it." She rummaged around in her large purse, came out with a wadded up tissue, dabbed at her eyes. She took out a small mirror, examined her face, deftly fixed her lipstick and powder. That done, she closed her purse and turned back to Skinny.

She picked up her glass of water and took a big swallow.

"Grover and Morgan have been selling property back and forth," she began, holding the glass of water in both hands, looking at Skinny over the rim of it, "between themselves. Most of the property is in the warehouse district, in the same area as the building that burned."

"So?" Skinny said, a little surprised by the abrupt change in direction, not knowing what Ruth was getting at but wanting to show that he was right with her.

"So each time they sell a piece, the price goes up considerably. And each time the price goes up, the appraisal goes up."

Skinny could tell from Ruth's expression that what she was telling him was important—important enough to be a violation of the loyalty she felt she owed her employer—but for the life of him, he couldn't understand why.

"So?" he said again.

Ruth pressed her lips together in a momentary frown, like a concerned teacher encountering an unreceptive student; then she put that behind her and went on.

"Skinny, you can borrow against the appraised value of property. All you need is a friendly banker to turn an appraisal into cash."

"What's the advantage to that? You have to repay a loan."

"No, you don't," Ruth replied, her tone surprisingly sharp. "You and I, *we* have to repay loans; but when you get to Morgan Barrett's level, your banker will roll a loan over for years. You just pay the interest." Ruth crossed her long legs and leaned forward over them. "You see what they're doing? They're artificially inflating the loan-value of their property. Maybe they're hoping to find a buyer at the inflated price. Or maybe they'll just let the bank foreclose on it. Why not? The property isn't worth what they've already gotten out of it through loans. But that's not the point. The point is, by flipping the property back and forth and having the appraisal raised each time, they're getting to a whole lot of money they really shouldn't have."

"How are they using the money?" Skinny asked, beginning to make connections, feeling the wheels starting to turn.

"That's what I don't know," Ruth replied, "not for certain. They spread the paperwork around so nobody in the office sees the whole picture. But my bet is, they're buying more property—including the warehouse that burned. Don't you see? If that is what they're doing, they *have* to have more to keep going. They're making new loans to pay the interest on the old ones."

"Is that legal?" Skinny asked, searching his memory for something, something right there he could not quite remember. "Flipping property to get higher appraisals?"

"You're asking *me* what's legal? *You're* the policeman."

Skinny did not really hear Ruth's reply because he was trying to understand what was bothering him, trying to make the connection he somehow knew he should make.

"Start at the beginning," he said, giving himself more time to think.

Ruth sat back and looked at him speculatively, her hazel eyes narrowed slightly, as if against smoke. She picked up her cigarette lighter and ran her thumb up the side of it, looking at it as she spoke.

"Grover does most of the legwork. He finds a piece of property—an abandoned factory, a vacant lot, an old warehouse—and he buys it. Then he sells it to Morgan. It's not that straightforward, of course, because they've set up subsidiary and independent companies."

"But the bottom line is," Skinny interjected, "Grover is selling the property to Morgan."

Ruth nodded.

"At a higher price than he bought it."

"Is that when they get the new appraisal?"

"Sometimes. Not always." Ruth used the lighter to light a new cigarette. "Sometimes they clean the property up first. They mow the grass or slap on a coat of paint."

"Then what?"

"*Then* they call the appraiser. They tell him what they think the property is worth, he sees what was paid for it, and more often than not, the appraisal comes in at the inflated price."

"So what was the party for last night?" Skinny asked, making the first leap. "If the bank will loan them money, why do they need investors?"

"It reduces their short-term debt, the amount they have to come up with every month. The investors buy into the property with them, and the interest payments go down by the amount of the investment—the investors don't expect a short-term return."

"Jesus," Skinny said, momentarily admiring the simplicity of it, but quickly coming back to the same question he had asked before. He could see how Morgan and Grover were raising lots of money, but the big question was, what were they using the money for?

"Maybe they'll just let the bank foreclose on it," Ruth had offered as one possibility.

But Skinny didn't buy that: it would ruin them at the bank, and it would ruin them with their investors, many of whom were their friends—he had seen that at the party.

"Or maybe they're hoping to find a buyer," Ruth had suggested as another possibility.

"Who would buy—?" Skinny started to ask himself, but he never finished the question because suddenly he knew the answers, both the answer to that question and to the one that had come before it: Karen had told him when they had been sitting on the side of the grassy embankment, looking down at her burning car.

"A package," she had explained, "is several small parcels put together to make one big parcel."

"No shit," Skinny very nearly said out loud.

"A package is much more valuable than the individual pieces that compose it. It makes big developments possible."

And if Morgan and Grover were floating loans to put together a package, every day was costing them money. Why hadn't he seen it before? If Stan Lee and his partner were holding them up, refusing to sell their warehouse, Morgan and Grover would *have* to find a way to get it. And what better way than to burn it down and to make it, for all practical purposes, useless?

"Can you get me a map?" Skinny asked. "Or a survey? Something that shows the property Morgan and Grover own in the area of the warehouse?"

"I'd have to draw one up," Ruth replied. She opened her purse again, rummaged through it, took out a pen and a small pad of paper. "I should have thought of that before," she said to herself as she scribbled herself a reminder.

"And Skinny'll need a list of the investors, who they are and how much they've invested."

"Skinny doesn't ask for much," Ruth remarked as she added the list to her note.

"That's only two things," Skinny said, Ruth's note to herself making him uneasy. In fact, a man had been killed, and the killer or killers very likely were very close. "You don't need to write them down."

"Ruth needs to write everything down," Ruth replied. She dropped the pad into her purse. "She'd forget her name if she didn't have it on her driver's license." She glanced at her watch as the waitress came up and put the check on the table. "I have to get back to the office."

"Skinny'll get this," Skinny volunteered, picking up the check and looking at it as he slid across the bench. When he was out of the booth and standing, he dug down into the pocket of his jeans and came out with a few wadded up bills. He examined them for denomination, then left two, only partially flattened, beside the check.

Ruth smiled an amused smile and went outside, Skinny right behind her.

"I'll call when I have the map and the list," she said. "I'll be as quick as I can."

For a long moment, Skinny just looked at her, hoping that she understood his concern but not wanting to frighten her.

"Be careful," was all he said.

Ruth smiled in reply and started off, going down the block, toward Grover's office.

Skinny watched her walk to the corner, then started back, the other way, to his truck. His truck was parked less than a block away, and when he got to it and opened the door, for some reason he glanced up. Not far away, in the central business district, the slick forty- and fifty-story buildings stood in a cluster. For the first time in his life, Skinny really looked at the buildings, studying them, seeing each one individually, knowing that each one was without doubt a big development made possible by someone assembling a package.

# 18

There were, Skinny knew, usually several ways to go about things, but Skinny being Skinny, the way he invariably chose was the way he perceived to be the most direct. So after spending a few minutes looking at the buildings downtown—and knowing that he would, at some point, have to meet Morgan Barrett, anyway—he got into his truck and drove to the foot of the tallest building on the skyline, having noted the building as Morgan Barrett's business address when, earlier that day, he had looked up his address at home. He parked right in front of the building, as near to the doors as he could get, put his police light up on the dash, and, ignoring the blaring horns of the cars he had blocked by simply stopping in the no-stopping lane, went stepping out across the broad plaza and in through the revolving doors.

Inside, crowded escalators went up from the concourse-style entrance to the huge, atrium-style lobby. Skinny checked at the information desk, caught the express elevator, and emerged in a two-story reception area with a whole wall made from plate glass, a curved staircase on one side and a receptionist's desk on the other. He winked at the receptionist and went on up the stairs, taking them two at a time.

The upstairs office was arranged around a central secretaries' bay, and Skinny toured the perimeter—looking in through the doors that were open, stopping to listen briefly at the doors that were closed—before he went up to the secretary he had noticed eyeing him with a curiosity that bordered on alarm.

"This is Skinny," he said, smiling brightly. "Skinny's here to see Morgan."

The secretary was very obviously uncertain what to make of him and smiled bravely; but she appeared about ready to spray him with mace.

"You sure aren't a Ruth," Skinny observed when she informed him stiffly that *Mr.* Barrett wasn't in. "Skinny'll come back," he concluded, and he went back downstairs, caught the elevator from there, and made it outside just as a city tow truck was backing up to his pickup.

Skinny jumped into his truck, backed up then pulled off, waving at the tow-truck driver as he passed him, secure in the knowledge that the license plate on his pickup was registered to a man doing fifteen-to-life in Angola. At the first stoplight he came to, he studied the position of the sun, decided his timing was right, and drove off to see Karen, yellow spots in the center of his vision.

The midday sun made the tree-filled neighborhood seem even more impressive, cool, pleasantly shaded, very private. Skinny went directly to Morgan Barrett's house, for some reason feeling more an outsider to the affluent area than he had earlier that morning, feeling more ill at ease than he was used to. He parked in front of the house, walked up the broad brick walkway, rang the bell, and listened as resonant tones sounded throughout the house.

An old black woman dressed in a white uniform opened the door. Her thin gray hair was pulled back tightly against her head, and the thin skin on her face was tight, shrunken over the prominent bones of her forehead and cheeks. She looked at Skinny curiously, then asked politely, "How may I help you, young man?"

"Skinny's here to see Karen," Skinny replied.

"Certainly," the old woman said without hesitation, and turned away from the door, leaving Skinny to close it, silently leading the way through the huge house.

The floor in the foyer was polished black flagstone beneath a ceiling that rose at least thirty feet over it. Directly in front of him, Skinny saw the broad staircase that curved away, right and left, and the sweeping lines of the banisters that did not quite follow the lines of the stairs, all the lines never intersecting, creating a sense of uninterrupted, flowing motion. Overhead, there was a large chandelier.

The flagstone gave way to plush blue carpet in a hallway that led past a study, a billiards room, a library, each of them very large rooms; on the left was a formal dining area next to a more casual area fitted out with overstuffed sofas and chairs. Beyond that, a glass wall gave a view of the ornate gardens outside.

"When was this house built?" Skinny asked, stopping to look at the garden.

"Mr. Barrett, Senior, built this house just after the war," the old woman replied, courteously stopping with him. "He called it his sweet-potato house."

Skinny looked at her questioningly. She did not look at him but seemed to know his question nevertheless.

"He made the money for it selling sweet potatoes to the

army," she explained. "He convinced the war people that yams were as good for you as spinach."

"He just happened to own a lot of yams, right?" Skinny guessed.

"By the time the war got going good, he did." The old woman smiled, then started to turn away.

"Is he still alive?" Skinny asked. "Mr. Barrett, Senior?"

"No," the old woman replied softly, sorrow in her expression. "He died three years ago this fall. He was an old man. It was time for him to go." She looked off, past the garden, then back. "Now Mr. Morgan owns all this."

There was regret in her tone, but whether it was regret for Morgan's ownership or for the passing of time, it was impossible to tell.

The old woman started down the hall again, and Skinny did not try to stop her with another question but let her go on.

The hallway dropped down two steps and became a covered brick walkway that went away from the house, back and at an angle, across a space of neatly trimmed lawn.

"Miss Karen is by the pool," the old woman said, and gestured for Skinny to go on, to the yellow and white pavilion he had noticed from the street.

Skinny nodded his thanks to the old woman and stepped past her, going on down the walkway, stopping once to look back at the house, for a moment wondering what it would have been like if his father had thought to farm yams.

The poolside pavilion looked much like an enormous gazebo. White trellis made up the walls, and for cover overhead, brightly colored canvas had been stretched over a steel frame that came to a point. Skinny went on in and saw the bar on the right, the comfortable arrangement of furniture for lounging, the large tan tiles that made up the floor; but he did not see Karen, so he went right on through, out into the bright sunshine that seemed even brighter after the deep shade under the pavilion.

The swimming pool meandered away, like a broad, deep section of friendly stream, the deck beside it wide in some places, narrow in others where large elephant-ear plants nearly touched the water. Skinny walked near the edge of the pool, and not far away he found Karen, stretched out on a partially raised lounge chair, naked, and all greased up for the sun. He stood very still, not certain what he should do—other, of course, than to look.

Karen had put the lounge chair at an angle to the pool, making the most of the sun, and the way Skinny had come up, he was looking the length of her, feet to head. The oil made her glisten all over; sunlight reflected silver-white on her shins and along the tops of her thighs. Skinny could see the line where she shaved her legs, where the fine, golden hairs began midway up her thighs, and he could see clearly the tangle of dark, curly hair between them. Her belly was flat, flat and soft, with a faint crease where the skin folded, and her breasts were made even more prominent, somehow vulnerable, by their whiteness, the triangular areas where her swimsuit had covered. Her eyes were closed, and despite the strong physical evidence imme- diately indicating the contrary, she still seemed very young, almost childlike in the way she had abandoned herself to the sun.

"Jesus," Skinny said softly, and looked away. "Damn," he said, and looked back.

Karen heard him, and she opened her eyes to see who it was; then she propped herself up on her elbows. She looked right at him and smiled slightly, holding his gaze confidently, making no attempt to cover herself whatsoever. When Skinny just stood there, she smiled again, a trace of amused triumph in her expression, and reached for the terry cloth robe on the chair next to her.

Skinny said, "You smell like some kind of tropical fruit." He unzipped his jacket a few inches and idly scratched at the hair on his chest.

Karen stood up and put on the robe.

He added, "It must be the oil."

Karen looked at him coolly, her eyes hard, bright blue in the sunshine, then she smiled, genuinely amused.

"You're certainly different," she said.

"There's only one Skinny," Skinny confirmed, glad that they had gotten that out of the way.

Karen used both hands to pull her hair out from the back of the robe, a movement that caused the robe to pull open all the way to her navel. She closed it and pulled the sash tight.

"I was going to call you today." She looked at the lounge chair as if she had forgotten something, then looked back at Skinny. "I wanted to apologize for the way I acted last night. It wasn't fair to get mad at you and your partner. I was pretty upset, I guess. Anyway, I'm sorry."

In the oversize robe, Karen looked very small, an appearance she exaggerated by seeming to slide down into it, ducking her head, forcing the robe up—a nice touch Skinny admired even as he saw through it. He already knew why she had put on the display of anger the night before. What he didn't know was what she had done with his gun.

"Forget it," he said, his shrewd eyes on hers. "It worked, and that's what counts, right?"

Karen did not acknowledge his comment in any way at all.

"Tell your partner for me, too," she said.

"Skinny'll tell him," Skinny agreed, deciding for the moment not to press it.

When Karen started toward him, he stepped to one side, into a large plant, to make room for her to pass.

"Stan Lee knows where you are," he said to her back, stepping forward, out of the plant. "He knows you're here. He was following you when you left this morning."

Karen stopped and looked back at him.

"How did he find me?"

Skinny innocently raised and dropped both his shoulders at once, conveying a puzzlement he did not really feel: he felt fairly certain Stan Lee had been following *him*, hoping he would do just what he did.

"I had a talk with him," Skinny said, and shrugged again, letting it go at that—not asking who might have been following *her*.

"Great," Karen said.

Skinny rubbed the tip of his chin.

High overhead, an airplane was passing, leaving a white trail.

When Skinny looked back, he saw that Karen had continued on and was most of the way to the pavilion. He followed her and was back in the shade as she went behind the bar and took out a half-gallon bottle of orange juice.

"You want some?" she asked, holding up the large bottle, holding it in both hands. When Skinny nodded, she poured two glasses full, put down the bottle, thought that over, then bent down to put the juice back in the refrigerator built into the bar.

Skinny picked up the glass nearest him and drained it before she had the door closed.

"Explain something to me," he said, quickly wiping his mouth with his hand, catching the overflow before it dripped down his chin.

"You want more?" Karen asked.

Skinny shook his head before he continued.

"Skinny understands the package—you already told him about that. You buy a bunch of small pieces of property and put them together to make one big piece; then you can build what you want, right?"

Karen nodded as she moved around the bar and pulled out a stool to face him.

"So in order to buy all those little pieces, you borrow as much as you can, and you convince people to invest. You guarantee them a return on their money. So what happens if you can't put the package together? Say something holds it up—or maybe you do get it all together but you can't sell it? What happens then?"

While Skinny had been asking his question, Karen had climbed up on the stool. She had crossed her legs Indian-style and leaned forward over them, as if she were sitting on a blanket spread out on the ground and not three feet up in the air.

"You just go ahead with some other project," she replied, taking a sip of her juice. "A smaller one."

"Like the one Grover showed pictures of at the party."

"Exactly. You start off thinking small and hope you can put together something better—either way, the investors *do* get repaid, with interest."

"But *you* don't make as much money," Skinny concluded, wiping up a wet ring on the bar, looking at his fingers, noting that Karen's explanation was not quite the same as the one she had opened with, when they had been sitting on the embankment watching her car burn. Then she had not been so calm, and the way she had described the consequences of an incomplete package had seemed more a major problem than an unfortunate annoyance. "So say it takes a year to know whether or not you have a salable package"—he looked at Karen for confirmation of his time estimate, and when she did not correct him, he went on— "and say it takes another year to build the smaller project and to lease or to sell it, then it's at least two years before you can even begin to repay the investors, *if* it all works out the way that you planned it."

"They understand that going in," Karen remarked, a slightly defensive edge to her tone.

"What's in it for them?" Skinny asked, feeling that he was on to something he hadn't before considered. "They leave their money with you for at least two years. They can't touch it, and they know the whole thing is a risk from the start. What makes them want to get into it at all?"

"A good salesperson," Karen interjected, smiling in a way that made it clear she was referring to herself.

But Skinny didn't buy that for a second. He had seen the people at the party, the potential investors, and he had seen both Karen and Grover work them, and that group—he would bet his last nickel on it—that group was concerned with what they got for their *money*.

"What's the return?" Skinny persisted. "The incentive? There has to be some bait on the hook."

"Are you thinking of investing?" Karen asked, smiling again, again not answering his question.

Skinny just looked at her, waiting.

"There *are* incentives," Karen replied finally, her easy humor giving way to displeasure.

"If nothing else works," a voice said, "we bribe them."

Both Karen and Skinny turned to see who had spoken, and they both saw Morgan Barrett coming toward them, stepping out of the dark entrance to the pavilion where, obviously, he had been for more than a few moments.

"How long have you been there?" Karen asked, a trace

of alarm in her tone which, apparently, she heard herself because she added, "You scared me," and smiled despite her disconcerted expression.

Skinny flicked a glance at her, curiously registering her alarm, then looked back at Morgan Barrett.

"Not long," Morgan said, replying to Karen but looking at Skinny. "I don't believe we've met."

Skinny started to say, "This is Skinny," but Karen beat him to it, saying exactly that and looking to Morgan as if introducing some tiresome topic. "He's a policeman. He's investigating the fire that burned down Grover's warehouse."

"Before it *was* Grover's warehouse," Skinny pointed out, stung by Karen's tone but not showing it.

Morgan Barrett was not quite as tall as Skinny, but he was tall enough that, despite his slouched posture, neither of them had to look more than a little up or down when they looked at each other. Above his high forehead, his hair was black and straight, parted on one side and combed straight across. Behind his black-framed glasses, his dark eyes were at the same time both alert and hard to catch, naturally evasive. For a man, he had a very long neck. He was wearing the same dark suit Skinny had seen him in that morning.

Skinny said, "Skinny just came from your office."

"I know," Morgan replied. He stood beside Karen, one arm behind her, placed casually along the back of her stool.

"Skinny wants to know how we convince our investors to invest," Karen said, looking up at Morgan. "I told him it takes a good salesperson."

"So I heard," Morgan remarked dryly.

Skinny looked from Karen to Morgan.

"Skinny wants to know that," he said, leaning against the bar, making a point of making himself comfortable, "and

Skinny wants to know why you and Grover flip property around to get higher appraisals."

The corners of Morgan's lips turned down in a look more annoyed than surprised.

"For precisely the reason you gave," he replied curtly. "To get higher appraisals. What does my business have to do with the fire?"

From the way he said, "my business," it was very obvious he meant, "my *personal* business."

"The fire was arson," Skinny answered evenly.

"Are you certain—?" Morgan began.

"It was deliberately set," Skinny went on, "which means someone had something to gain."

Morgan held Skinny's gaze a moment, then his eyes slipped away again.

"I see," he said vaguely. He took off his glasses and from his hip pocket took out a white handkerchief to clean them, wiping first one lens then the other with a circular motion, looking down the whole time at his hands.

Skinny waited patiently, watching the show.

Karen looked off, as if at some point in the distance, curiously detached.

Morgan finally put his glasses back on, refolded the handkerchief, put it back in his pocket.

"Was the fire in the warehouse set by the same person who set fire to your car?" he asked Karen.

Karen did not seem about to reply, so Skinny answered for her.

"Skinny thinks so," he said. "She's not so sure. When we nail somebody for one, we can ask about the other."

Morgan continued to look at Karen, and Karen continued to look off, a lack of response Morgan for some reason seemed to enjoy. Skinny had the sense something was going on he knew nothing about, something that was, at the moment, working well for Morgan.

"So tell me a little more about why you and Grover flip property," he said. "There has to be more to it."

"Not so much, really," Morgan replied, reluctantly looking away from Karen. "There's nothing illegal about it, if that's what you're hoping." He grasped the back of Karen's stool and leaned on that arm. He put one highly polished black shoe in front of the other. "There are two ways to demonstrate that the value of a property has increased," he began, his tone slightly bored, as if he were explaining something he really shouldn't have to explain. "You can either put together a list showing recent sales of comparable properties in the same area and an accounting of the money that's been spent on improvements; or you can sell it. A sale is self-proving, much preferable to lists and accountings: the sale price is, in fact, what the piece is worth on the market."

"But once you sell it," Skinny noted, "it's not yours anymore. So what's the difference?"

"The difference comes after you buy it back. Then you go to an appraiser and tell him what you paid for it—and what the property sold for previously." Morgan paused, his expression smug, more than a little amused. "It gives him something to work with."

"He only knows about *one* prior sale," Karen said suddenly, no longer detached but right there. "He doesn't do a title search, so he only knows about the most recent sale. He—"

"He has access to any information he wants," Morgan corrected her, his tone deliberate and forceful, patronizing. "Once a sale is recorded, it becomes public information, available to anyone who cares to look it up."

"Which *he* doesn't."

"They are, for the most part, very busy men," Morgan

conceded, giving Karen a look that was as pleased as hers was angry before he glanced back at Skinny. "But it doesn't really matter. The sales take place between wholly—*legally*—independent entities."

When Karen did not say anything else, Skinny surmised, "And once you have the higher appraisal, you go to the bank for a loan."

Morgan moved his chin down and raised his eyebrows in a way that showed he concurred.

"That way," he added, not looking at Karen but seeming to speak for her benefit, "one's own money is at risk only for a very short period of time."

Skinny looked at Karen as he considered the sequence, sale, resale, appraisal, seeing the sense to it but not really accepting it. Even if it was completely legal, which, somehow, he doubted, there was a trickiness to it that made it appear sleazy; and if he saw it that way, how would the people view it who had money invested?

"So how do you convince your investors to invest?" he asked, going back to his first question. "What's in it for them?"

Morgan waited a few beats before he replied, as if waiting for Karen to speak.

"Simply put," he said finally, "what's in it for them is cash. We pay them to invest."

To Skinny that made no sense at all.

"Wait a minute," he began, recalling what Ruth had told him, that the whole point of the flips was to raise money. Assuming that was the case—and he could see no other reason for all their maneuverings—why would they give it away at the outset? "Wait a minute," he said again, but another thought suddenly struck him: Karen had paid cash for her rent and deposit. He had read that in her file at the complex. And her car was brand-new. "You pay them to invest?" he asked dumbly.

"At some banks," Morgan replied, "they give you a toaster or a microwave oven when you open a new account. We simply make our incentive more liquid."

"How much do you give them?"

"It varies, of course, according to how much they invest."

"According to how much they *borrow*," Karen added.

Skinny did not understand that, but he waited to ask another question, preferring to study what was happening between Karen and Morgan, the antagonism and resultant anger.

"They sell off pieces based on the inflated appraisals," Karen went on.

"Based on what we anticipate the value of a unit to be," Morgan corrected her.

"It amounts to the same thing," Karen snapped, "as you well know." Her eyes bored into Morgan, and when he glanced away, smirking, she looked back at Skinny, her eyes hot and hard. She started to say something, reconsidered, got down from the stool. "I'm going to get dressed," she said. She flashed another angry look at Morgan before she moved past Skinny, leaving without looking back.

Both Skinny and Morgan watched her go, neither of them making a move to stop her.

After Karen had gone, Morgan continued to look at the doorway, his expression pensive and vacant, which gave Skinny an opportunity to study him again—not that there was a whole lot to see that he hadn't already noted. What interested Skinny most was what he didn't fully understand, the exchange that had just taken place, the way Morgan had played out his line and how Karen had risen to the bait, snapping and fighting once hooked. It seemed to Skinny that there was some sort of contest taking place between them, a game or a battle, and he was curious to learn the rules and what was at stake.

He said, "So fuck her if she can't take a joke," watching to see how Morgan responded, knowing he had said the right thing when Morgan smiled thinly, obviously amused.

"My sentiments exactly," he said, and his eyes flicked to Skinny before they moved off again.

"What made her so mad?" Skinny asked. "Skinny doesn't get it."

Morgan looked at the stool where Karen had sat, then he looked at the thin watch on his wrist. He raised and dropped his eyebrows, as if Karen's anger were unfathomable to him, too.

"I have to get back to my office," he said. He pulled out the cuff of his shirt, carefully aligning that cuff with the cuff of his coat. "If you have any further questions, feel free to call me."

"Okay," Skinny said easily, raising and dropping both his shoulders at once, playing out his line, too. "Skinny needs to use the phone."

Morgan absently indicated the phone on the wall behind the bar, then he left, too, leaving Skinny alone in the poolside pavilion.

Skinny went behind the bar and helped himself to more juice, picked up the phone and dialed the number he wanted.

"Fucking sweet potatoes," he said, looking around appreciatively, stretching out the long cord on the phone, stretching out himself on a lounge chair, making himself comfortable for what he knew was going to be a lengthy conversation.

# 19

Where Karen was staying upstairs was a suite of rooms every bit as large as her apartment in the complex, and as she spoke on the phone, using the private line that came with the Barrett house's more-than-generous guest accommodations, she walked back and forth, from the sitting room window to the window in the bedroom, with every step enjoying the feel of the luxurious carpet that ran from one room to the next.

Karen had seen Morgan leave the poolside pavilion, and she was curious as to what had happened to Skinny: there was still time to catch another hour of sun, but she had no desire to run into Skinny again, not when she felt so confident she had left him with just the impression she wanted him to have.

She said into the phone, "I don't know who it is, Grover. You have to decide that." She moved aside the thin, gauze-like curtains that covered the bedroom window so she could see out more clearly. "I just know there's a leak. Someone in the office is giving out information—and you can bet it's not me."

Karen let the thin curtain fall back into place.

"No, I don't think it's you, either." She walked over and flopped down on the huge bed, heedless of the oil she was getting on the flawlessly white comforter. "The policeman investigating the fire asked me about the flips, that's how I know."

She moved back until her head was resting on the pillows.

"Whether or not he's been spending time researching titles, which I doubt, don't you think someone had to tell him what to look for in the first place?"

On a sudden impulse, Karen rolled over onto her stomach and reached beneath the bed. She pulled out her small leather suitcase, put it on the bed, sat up beside it.

"Well, work backward," she suggested. "Other than Morgan and you and me, who knows about the flips?"

Slowly, she unzipped the bag, using both hands, holding the phone by pressing it between her shoulder and ear.

"Even if what we're doing isn't illegal, Grover, a leak could still be disastrous—you know that. Do you want us in a bid war with someone who knows all our plans? Or do you want a property owner to realize he has a piece of a potential package?"

She opened the bag and looked around inside it.

"You pay your employees enough," she added. "The least they can do is to keep their mouths shut."

She opened the bag wider, saw what she was looking for, glanced around cautiously, as if someone else might be in the room.

"Yes," she agreed. "Ruth was the first person to cross my mind, too."

Taking it by the black rubber grips, Karen pulled Skinny's long silver revolver out of the bag.

"I'd fire her."

She held the revolver up, close to her face.

"And I'd fire her *today*."

It took Skinny quite a while to explain to Mike Theriot what he had learned. Aside from the normal crimps in conversation between them, this particular explanation was made even more difficult by the fact that Skinny did not as yet have a complete understanding of events himself. He was still replaying the exchange between Karen and Morgan, sorting it out in his mind, and he was just beginning to realize how many questions he still had for them both—but he did know just exactly what he wanted from Mike Theriot.

"Jesus Christ in a wheelbarrow," he nearly shouted. "Are you listening? It's only two things. Two things." He jumped up from the lounge chair and stepped away from it, realizing only when his neck twisted to one side that he had reached the end of the cord on the phone. He stepped back the other way, moving but giving the cord no slack whatsoever. "First, you call up Motor Vehicles and get the complete registration on Karen's car. That'll give you the name of the dealership where she bought it. Then you go out there—"

"What if she bought it in Houston?" Mike Theriot asked, his tone earnest, unable to resist, knowing it was exactly the sort of question that drove Skinny right up the wall. "Or Atlanta?"

"What?" Skinny asked in reply, incredulous. "Your phone doesn't go that far? The car is *registered* in *Louisiana*."

"Okay," Mike Theriot conceded. "Just checking."

Skinny made a face into the phone.

"You go out to the dealership—or you call them—and you ask how she paid for her car."

"What does that have to do with anything?"

"It's important," Skinny replied. "Trust Skinny on this one."

Mike Theriot grunted doubtfully, a sound Skinny chose to ignore.

"Second, you call the Central Appraisal Bureau, and you find out the names of appraisers who work the warehouse district. You go to see one or two of them. Ask if they know Grover or Morgan and if they've ever done work for them."

"Do I ask about these 'flips'?" Mike Theriot asked, consulting his notes.

"Jesus Christ, Theriot, of course you ask about the flips. What else *would* you ask them? What they do on their day off? Feel them out. See whether or not they already know what's going on. See what they have to say."

"Okay," Mike Theriot agreed, conscientiously writing down the questions he should ask, underlining the part about *feel them out*, "but I may not be able to get to it today. We're shorthanded up here, you know."

"Skinny knows," Skinny said, standing still for a moment before he stepped back behind the bar.

"You could at least do part of this yourself," Theriot suggested. "It might save some time."

Skinny shook his head into the phone.

"Skinny thought about that. He can't." He picked up the two glasses where they had been left on the bar and put them into the sink. "This one is going to court, Theriot. Defense counsel finds out Skinny was working while he was on suspension, they'll find a way to get everything he touched disallowed. They'll claim false representation. The flips and the car, they're both recorded information, and we need the records to make a case. But Skinny can talk to people, that's no problem—people can be made to talk again in court."

"You can talk, all right," Mike Theriot agreed, adding Skinny's two things to the list of other things he had to do.

"Do the best you can with it," Skinny added. "Skinny'll talk to you later."

After he hung up the phone, Skinny turned on the water in the sink and rinsed out the glasses he and Karen had used. He wasn't in any hurry to leave since all he had planned was to go back to his truck and to wait again where he had waited early that morning, watching the house, watching out for Stan Lee; so he went back to the lounge chair where he had been sitting before, adjusted it to his liking, and waited a while there in the poolside pavilion instead.

# 20

Karen was no stranger to guns. During deer season and duck season, there had always been rifles and shotguns around her father's house. Just the steel-and-oil smell of guns made her think of her father, but she preferred not to think about him now because, as she saw it, he was directly responsible for her present situation. He had misled her. He had made her believe he was wealthy when, in fact, he had hardly been more than comfortable—and he had left her to fend for herself. Still, as she figured out how to get the revolver to open—she wanted to be very sure it was loaded—thoughts of him crept into her efforts.

She pushed on the cylinder release, held the revolver up, and shook it roughly. The cylinder dropped open, and the +P+ hollow-point bullets fell into her lap.

"It's all in the touch," her father had told her one time as he had taken his shotgun apart for cleaning, gently placing the various parts on his desk. "The touch and the sequence."

"Right," Karen said bitterly.

She put the revolver down, picked up the cartridges, and examined them, surprised to find that one had been fired.

She lay back again, her head on the pillows, and curiously compared the empty casing to a live round. She liked the live one much better, she decided. She liked its solid little weight and the way it seemed to hold the warmth from her hand. She liked its potential.

She dropped the bullets beside the revolver and got up, going back to the window to look out again.

She would be glad to be rid of Ruth, she realized. She had never liked her, which made them equal that way, at least, since Ruth had never liked her, either. Ruth was resentful of her, of course, resentful of her looks and of her connections—and her remarks had always been a little too barbed, her pretense of dry humor a little too thin.

*Good riddance,* she thought, checking the sun and frowning slightly because she did not know whether she could go back to the pool.

But she did know that the interview with Skinny had gone well. She had been able to set the tone of the conversation, portraying herself as a victim, simply by playing to Morgan and his infuriatingly smug conceit.

*That shit,* she thought, a slow, satisfied smile crossing her face.

Skinny would be more than a little curious about what had made her angry. He had to be. And if he wasn't, she would keep after him until he was and the thrust of his investigation would deflect slightly, from the fire itself to the business that had prompted it. Once he was following the leads she gave him, she would take him into a mire of details, details just revealing enough to make Morgan squirm when he tried to explain them.

Her smile broadened.

And *then* she would tell Morgan about her package. She would take him to Commander's for lunch, and she would explain it carefully and at length. She would lay it out so he saw clearly how she had beaten him at every turn and how she had used *his* money to make herself rich. She would see how his crabmeat salad went down with *that*.

*Touch and sequence,* she thought, thinking again of her father, of what he would say.

She left the bedroom window and went back to the window in the sitting room, changing her angle of view.

But first she had to take care of one last detail of her own.

Skinny was getting close, she knew that. He was clever, and he was asking all the right questions. She could not afford to underestimate him for a minute. The bad break had come, of course, when there had been someone in the warehouse when she had lured Stan Lee out and Rick had set the fire—the police investigation of the simple arson she had intended would have been perfunctory, quickly concluded, a matter left to the insurance company to settle. The fact that Stan Lee's partner had been inside the building had been just plain bad luck. It had been just plain good luck, however, when she had found Skinny's revolver and had stashed it in her bedroom before he had waken up. And when she had heard Skinny say he was certain it was Stan Lee who had broken into her apartment, she had known that the good luck had held because she had seen right away that she had the solution she needed, the neat closure.

*Now, if I could just get some more sun,* she thought, starting to move away from the window again but stopping herself, constructing a scene in her mind.

Since Skinny was certain it was Stan Lee who had broken into her apartment, he must have guessed that it was Stan Lee who had taken his gun. So if Rick Trask was found shot and the revolver was nearby, who *wouldn't* conclude that Stan Lee had caught up with the arsonist and killed him for revenge? It made perfect sense. With Skinny's revolver supposedly in his possession, he had the means. He certainly had the motive—and if Stan Lee was following her, so much the better: she would even place him near the scene and give him the opportunity. All she had to do now was to figure out the place.

In her mind, it was dark, of course, dark and still. She was looking for Rick in a large but enclosed space, looking around, trying to see, listening for his footsteps but hearing only her own. Suddenly she could feel the weight of the revolver in her hands. She could see its shiny silver surface, as if it were gathering light rather than just reflecting it, as it had been when she had first seen it on her kitchen floor. The shadows seemed to move.

She felt his presence before she actually saw him, then she turned a corner and there he was, leaning against a post or a wall, his hands in the pockets of his cheap cotton jacket, that hard-cocky expression on his face.

The revolver seemed weightless, moving as if on its own, floating up.

Her grip tightened.

Karen quickly turned away from the window. Unaware that she was doing so, she tucked her hair back over her ear, her fingers moving slowly, her eyes unfocused but fixed.

# 21

Ruth had never been fired before. Of necessity, she had started working before she had graduated from high school, and while in the twenty-plus years since then she had both quit jobs and been laid off, nothing had quite prepared her for the desolation of being suddenly, irrevocably fired.

She did not know quite what to do.

She cleaned out her desk, separating her own small possessions—her desk calendar, small vase for the single flower she sometimes bought for herself, small placard that read *Do you want to talk to the boss or to someone who knows what's going on around here?*—from the various supplies the company had provided her for work. She put her things in a copy-paper box, the company's things on top of the desk, and the things she could not quite decide about on the floor. She stopped sorting long enough to light one of her long, thin cigarettes, careful not to look around, not to catch the eyes of the other women in the office. She blew the smoke at the ceiling, then quickly looked down, feeling the start of tears and not wanting anyone to see. She pretended to consider a box of paper clips and furtively dabbed at her eyes with the wadded-up tissue she was holding in one hand.

Grover had been furious, there was no doubt about that. She had never even seen him angry before, never more than a little flustered, and suddenly there he was, at her desk, leaning over and taking the papers right out of her hands. He had reached over and snapped off her computer.

"Pack up your personal things," he had said. "I want you out of here today."

He had started to leave, but as an afterthought he had turned back and leafed through the papers on her desk. He had pulled open her top drawer and gone through it.

Ruth had sat back, too stunned to react, and more than anything else, she recalled, at that moment she had noticed how he smelled of soap and talcum powder, as if he were fresh out of the shower. She had seen the surprisingly coarse hairs on the back of his hand and admired his flawlessly white, starched cuff.

Suddenly, she had remembered the note she had written to herself, the one Skinny had warned her about writing, reminding herself to draw a map showing the property Grover and Morgan owned in the warehouse district and to make a list of the current project's investors. The material was already in her purse, but she had left the note in a drawer. She thought about it just as Grover had found it. He had glanced at the pink message slip, then he had read it, immediately understanding what it meant; and the look he had given her was what had hurt most of all. In his expression, she had seen anger, disappointment, hurt, and, finally, disgust. And as Ruth viewed it, he was right to feel all those things. She felt them herself—those things and more: she felt desolate, very much alone and uncertain. She felt she had nowhere to turn.

She put her cigarette in the ashtray and leaned down to the bottom drawer of her desk.

"A man died in the fire," she reminded herself just as Skinny had reminded her.

*Skinny*.

"You weren't just telling him things?" Grover had asked, reading the note she had written to herself, incredulity mixed with his disgust. "You were actually taking things out of the office?"

He had torn the pink message slip to pieces and tossed it at the trashcan; but most of the pieces had gone onto the floor.

Skinny had let something slip, no doubt about it. Not that it mattered. Not now.

She had some money in savings, not very much but enough to get by on until she found another job; most of her bills were current. She'd be okay. She'd find a way to cover the gap in her resumé—she felt certain Grover would not give her a reference, if she ever got up the nerve even to ask for one . . .

At the back of the bottom drawer she found the good-luck card that had been given her just before she had had the surgery on her eyes. It was signed by everyone in the office. She felt a surge of emotion and quickly slipped the card into the box with her things.

She sat up straight, picked up her cigarette and just held it, having finished the last of the sorting.

It hadn't been a bad place to work, she decided, momentarily detached from her thoughts. The work itself had been interesting. The pay had been fair—the coffee had been bad, but the coffee had been bad every place she had ever worked. She had made some new friends. . . . Overall, there had been some pretty good moments.

Ruth felt the start of another surge of emotion and quickly put out her cigarette, picked up her box, and left before the sadness hit her, leaving behind the office and the people with whom she had spent most of her time for over four years.

After a while, Skinny had been bored just sitting in the pool house, so he had finally left there and gone to sit in his truck; but a while later he had gotten bored there, too, feeling he was doing no good whatsoever, so he had found his way to a convenience store and bought himself a cup of coffee in a Styrofoam cup and a can of Vienna sausage. He dunked the end of each little sausage in the coffee before he ate it, chewing slowly and idly trying to figure out what he should do.

He pretty much had the bases covered, he realized, satisfied with the progress that had been made. He had more questions, of course, but what he had to do now was to wait. He disposed of the can the sausage had come in and, because the trash container was near a pay phone, decided to check in with Ruth. When he was told that Ruth no longer worked in the office, it took him a moment to put it together, to realize what probably had happened.

"She was fired?" he asked.

"Yes," the woman answered reluctantly, her voice strained.

"Damn," he said, before he thought to ask for Ruth's address at home.

"Shit," he said after he had hung up the phone.

*       *       *

Ruth's apartment was in the Irish Channel, not far from uptown, in an old Victorian house that had been divided up into three separate apartments. Ruth had taken the rear apartment because she liked the big double-hung windows that looked out into the brick courtyard that was, for all practical purposes, overgrown, filled with what she supposed were swamp-type plants, vines, bushes, and small trees of every description. She liked the old glass in the windows, the bubbles and the imperfections in it. She liked the way she could see at least seven different shades of green.

Ruth had gone home from the office, put the copy-paper box in the hall closet, out of sight, and had sat in her favorite chair. She had looked out at the plants and had watched the chameleons scrambling along the branches, the male lizards stopping every once in a while to puff out their pink necks. She was just sitting there when she heard the knock at her door and got up to answer it, not really expecting anything, just doing it reflexly; and she was both surprised and not surprised to see Skinny, a big bag of groceries in one hand and a six-pack of root beer in the other.

"So it's Skinny," she said, mustering a smile.

"It's Skinny," Skinny affirmed, his expression at the same time both serious and concerned. He held her gaze until she looked away. "Skinny came to make you a pizza," he said. "Pizza always makes Skinny feel better when he's down."

For what seemed a long time, Ruth did not reply in any way at all. She looked one way, then another, her eyes lowered, and put her hands in the pockets of her skirt.

Skinny just stood there, feeling bad, his lips pressed tightly together, feeling that maybe pizza hadn't been such a good idea, after all.

Then Ruth stepped out onto the landing and took him by

the arm, turning back toward her apartment as she did so, leading him inside.

"Pizza makes Ruth feel better, too," she said.

"Skinny's pretty sure it's the anchovies that do it," Skinny added quickly. "He got a big can of the good ones." He stopped in the hallway as Ruth closed the door. "It takes about an hour."

"Ruth has an hour," Ruth said. "She's on vacation."

Skinny started to say something, thought better of it, went on into the kitchen and unloaded the groceries onto the counter. That done, he turned on the oven, checked to be sure it had lit, and began to go through the cabinets, leaving the doors open as he looked in each one. He found a mixing bowl about the size he had been searching for, wiped it out with his hand, turned around and put it into the oven.

"You have to have a warm bowl to start," he asserted. "*You* should warm up the milk. A cup and a half."

Ruth accepted the role of assistant, helping out as directed as Skinny made dough, putting the ingredients together with a well-practiced efficiency. Ten minutes later, they had to wait a half hour.

"It takes that long for the dough to rise," Skinny explained.

"In that case," Ruth said, turning to wash her hands at the sink, "*you* should get the sous-chef a glass of wine—it's in the refrigerator."

Skinny took out the wine, poured Ruth a glass, opened a root beer for himself. He leaned back against the counter, waiting for Ruth, knowing the time the dough needed to rise would give them time to talk. There was no need to force it.

Ruth dried her hands, picked up the wine, and took a sip. For a moment, she seemed to consider the taste.

"Thank you," she said finally, and looked right at Skinny. "Thank you for coming."

Briefly, Skinny held her gaze, then his eyes flicked away.
"It's Skinny's fault, isn't it, that you were fired?"
Ruth shook her head slightly.
"Ruth is a big girl, Skinny," she replied, her voice firm.
"You may recall that I phoned you. I knew the risks."
Skinny's eyes came back to hers.
"But I'm the one who spilled the beans."
Ruth glanced away thoughtfully.
"Yes," she replied finally, honestly, but without malice or
anger. She rubbed her thumb on the lip of her glass. "I don't
know how else they could have found out. I was very careful."
She took another sip from her wine. "Grover didn't ask
any questions. He already knew—he just came in and told
me to leave."

Skinny remembered how clever he had felt when he had
said to Morgan Barrett, "And Skinny wants to know about
the flips." He remembered how Morgan's expression had
been more annoyed than surprised.

"Will you be able to find another job?" he asked.

"I can type, Skinny," Ruth replied. "I can always find
work."

It was Skinny's turn to glance away, and he did, seeing
that the dough was already beginning to rise, feeling a
sadness tinged with anger, a sense of helplessness and
unfairness.

"Skinny sometimes does things he regrets later," he said.
"He just does things. He doesn't always think."

Ruth saw what he was trying to say, and it touched her.
There was a fundamental honesty about Skinny, a lack of
hesitation between thought and act, that made his character
almost transparent. He *was* what he was doing and saying,
without guile or pretense, and at that moment it was obvious
he was taking on far more than his share of any blame.

She put down her glass, went up beside him, and took his hand in hers.

"Do you know what got me the most?" she said, and gave his hand a squeeze. When he shook his head, she went on, "It was seeing how the other women in the office acted after Grover fired me. Some were glad to see me go, certainly, and others were genuinely hurt, I think. But whatever they felt about me, behind that, every one of them was afraid. I could see it in the way they snuck looks at me, as if I had been diagnosed with some terrible illness. They were afraid because the same thing could happen to them. And so what, Skinny? Don't you see? So what? The fear of its happening is worse than when it really does. I'll find another job. I'll be all right—better off than they are, in fact. If there's anyone *really* to blame, it's whoever set fire to the warehouse. I wasn't wrong to try to help you find out who it was." She smiled warmly. "In the meantime, my friends come by. I get homemade pizza, made for me right in my own kitchen . . ." She reached out and touched Skinny on the cheek. "I get a few days off." She leaned forward and kissed him, lightly at first, then harder.

Skinny put his arms around her and pulled her in closer.

"What about my pizza?" Ruth asked a few minutes later, at the first opportunity.

Skinny ran his hands up and down her sides.

"You're almost as bony as Skinny," Skinny said in reply. He slipped away from her, quickly put the dough for the pizza in the refrigerator, took her hand, and led her back toward her bedroom. "We're *both* too bony for all that kitchen-floor stuff," he added.

"Speak for yourself," Ruth objected, feigning a little resistance.

"You serious?"

"We could compromise on the carpet," she suggested, showing just the hint of a smile.

Skinny glanced at the carpet in the living room, then looked back at her.

"Skinny's not too skinny for carpet," he agreed, matching her smile.

# 22

Ruth and Skinny spent a good portion of the rest of the afternoon on the carpet, then they did finally move to Ruth's bed. By the early evening, however, their other appetites won out and they agreed to get up to finish making the pizza.

"Ruth should get fired more often," Ruth said as she got up.

"Skinny's got rug burns," Skinny observed, sitting up, rotating his arms to examine his elbows. He looked up and smiled brightly. "But they were worth it."

"Ruth's got rug burns, too," Ruth confided, "but they're in other places."

Ruth put on a robe and found another one for Skinny.

Before he put it on, Skinny interestedly examined his knees.

In the kitchen, Ruth poured herself more wine while Skinny kneaded the dough on the counter.

"Skinny'll make two small pizzas to start," Skinny said, "then two more to cook while we're eating the first ones."

Ruth kissed him lightly on the side of the neck and moved

past him, out of the kitchen. When she came back, her makeup was renewed.

Skinny was adding the topping.

"Black olives, tomatoes, cheese, anchovies, green peppers, and bologna," he said proudly. He saw Ruth's expression when he mentioned the bologna, and he added, "Wait'll you taste it."

"This is taking longer than an hour," Ruth remarked.

"Skinny was interrupted," Skinny said.

He put the first two pizzas into the oven and set the timer. He saw the root beer he had opened earlier and took a long swallow. It was warm in the kitchen, almost hot, and when he rinsed his hands, he rinsed his face, too, finding when he came up for air Ruth right there with a paper towel.

Ruth handed him the towel, waited for him to use it, then handed him the papers she had retrieved from her purse.

The top sheet was much larger than the typewritten sheets it enclosed, but as soon as Skinny saw the thick, folded wad of paper, he knew what it was.

"You got it, anyway?" he asked, accepting the papers but just holding them, his tone a mix of incredulity and residual guilt.

"Ruth got it," Ruth said triumphantly, flashing a smile. "The ownerships of property *and* the list of investors." She took back the papers and spread them out on the counter, smoothing them down with the heel of her hand. She put the typewritten sheets to one side. "This is called a Sanbourne map," she explained, her tone tinged with excitement, giving the large sheet one final rub. "It shows the buildings in each city block—this one is of the warehouse district. Pretty interesting, isn't it?"

Skinny wasn't that familiar with the warehouse district, and it took him a moment to orient himself, to understand what he was seeing. At the bottom of the map, there were parallel and noodlelike lines that indicated the Mississippi river bridges, inbound and outbound, and all the approach ramps; at the top of the map, there were large squares that indicated the tower buildings that made up downtown. The top and the bottom of the sheet were relatively uncomplicated, but between those easily read landmarks, there were literally hundreds of little irregularly shaped rectangles, each one filled up with abbreviated, lettered information. To Skinny, it looked like some complex board game. He wanted to ask for the dice. Ruth had marked several of the small squares with an *X*, and as he watched, she took out a pencil and began to shade them.

"I meant to do this earlier," she said, glancing at Skinny long enough to smile, "but I haven't had time." She held the pencil low to the paper and shaded with the side of the lead. "This is the property Morgan and Grover owned or had options to buy at the time of the fire."

As Ruth shaded, Skinny made a quick count of the squares she had marked. There were twelve in all, including what had been Stan Lee's shop, and there were, apparently, two alleys. Taken together, the buildings and the alleys made up nearly a whole city block.

"Jesus," he said to himself, thinking of the huge amount of money involved.

As Ruth's shading became darker, the shape of a large rectangle began to emerge, and Skinny compared it to the other large rectangles at the top of the map, seeing that it was smaller than some but larger than others—certainly large enough for a good-sized development. He began to really understand what Karen had meant when she had explained assembling a package. It was like putting together a puzzle, fitting small squares together to make up one big one.

Ruth stopped using the pencil and switched to a marker.

"This," she said, holding the marker poised before she outlined the last square in red, "is the warehouse that burned."

The contrast in colors—the orange-red against the lead-gray—caught Skinny's eye before he constructed the whole picture, making the leap to the final square's importance.

"Jesus Christ," he said out loud because he saw that without the red square, without Stan Lee and Mitchell's warehouse, the rectangle more closely resembled a thick-sided horseshoe. It was incomplete, practically useless. There was no way to work around it.

Impulsively, he stepped forward and picked up the map, taking it right out from under Ruth's hand.

"Sorry," he said, holding the large sheet up high, looking more closely, in his mind picturing the buildings the squares represented. Most of the buildings were brick, he knew, and most of them had at one time or another been warehouses. They were low and broad, and they all had flat roofs.

"Are you sure this is right?" Skinny asked.

"Each one I marked had its own separate file," Ruth replied. "I'm positive."

Skinny's gaze was steady on the map. There was a motive, graphically illustrated, any jury would see: Stan Lee and Mitchell had been in the way.

His gaze flicked to Ruth, and he smiled.

"No shit," he said.

He put down the map and picked up the list of investors.

"That was easier to get," Ruth explained. "There's a mailing list for the investors. I just printed it out onto paper rather than labels."

The list was longer than Skinny had expected, six typewritten pages, but he took the time to read every name, reading some of them twice when they seemed somehow familiar.

"Who are all these people?" he asked. "Where do they find them?"

"Grover comes up with most of them," Ruth replied. "He goes to a lot of parties."

Each page of the list was arranged in three columns; the names were arranged alphabetically, top to bottom. Skinny looked over the list again and stopped when he came to *H:* Karen Kincaid Hodges.

"How much did Karen invest?"

Ruth shook her head side to side in a way that showed she was uncertain.

"I don't know." She took a cigarette from the pocket of her robe and lit it, seemingly all in one motion. "The minimum investment is fifty thousand dollars."

Skinny flipped back through the list, seeing the names of all those people with that much money to spare.

"Most of them borrow to buy in," Ruth added, as if reading his thoughts. "They take out a mortgage to buy one of the condominiums."

Skinny stopped flipping the pages and looked at Ruth.

"So they're just paying a note?"

"Right," Ruth affirmed. "All they have to have, really, is decent credit and enough cash for a down payment."

Skinny looked back at the list, but he was no longer seeing the names. Ruth's mention of cash had triggered his memory, and he began to replay what Morgan Barrett had said about a cash *bonus*.

"At some banks," Morgan had explained, "they give you a toaster or a microwave oven when you open a new account. We simply make our incentive more liquid."

So if the investors committed to a long-term loan to buy in, Skinny figured, following the sequence, they got cash back right away.

*That's a pretty good incentive, all right*, Skinny thought, acknowledging the sense to it, realizing how well Morgan had answered his question. *It covers the cost of the down payment and puts a little change in their pockets.*

"What came next?" Skinny asked himself, trying to remember the conversation exactly, knowing he was on the right track.

"The amount of the bonus varies," Morgan had added, "according to how much they invest."

"According to how much they *borrow*," Karen had snapped, her anger right there, very nearly explosive.

"According to how much they borrow," Skinny repeated to himself. "According to how much they invest."

Skinny did not immediately grasp the importance of the distinction, and he tossed the phrases back and forth in his mind, knowing that whatever he was missing was significant enough to have spurred Karen's anger. His eyes flicked about as he repeated the words, his lips moving silently.

If you borrow to invest, he finally figured, you would want cash back; but if you're not borrowing, you probably don't need it.

*That makes sense*, Skinny thought, *but then what had made Karen so angry?*

Skinny's gaze fixed on the map where he had left it on the counter, caught by Ruth's shadings, the orange-red all but surrounded by lead-gray.

And suddenly, he knew.

"She borrowed to buy into a package that could not be completed," he said out loud, the words coming out even before he realized what he was saying. "Not without Stan Lee and Mitchell's warehouse. And if she didn't put the package together, she'd have to pay thirty years for nothing."

Ruth looked at him questioningly, not following the leap he had made but feeling the change in his mood.

"You just got it, didn't you?" she asked.

Skinny glanced at her, and he nodded.

"Skinny got it," he said.

He stepped forward, picked up the phone on the end of the counter, quickly punched in a number.

"Who are you calling?" Ruth asked, a little perturbed that he wasn't telling her first.

"Theriot," Skinny replied, and moved the receiver up to his ear. "Skinny wants to be sure he got it *right*." He glanced again at the map. "The son of a bitch *better* have done Skinny's homework."

# 23

Rick Trask was surprised to hear from Karen, that was for sure. For three days, she had been avoiding him, not returning his calls, not coming by, and suddenly there she was on the phone, calling him at home, just like old times.

"Do you know what I'm doing right now?" she began coyly, not really meaning it, though, he could tell from her tone, just using it as a sort of hello.

"Where have you been?" he snapped. "Other than avoiding me?"

"Of course I've been avoiding you," she snapped right back, as if she had known he would say what he had. "Do *you* think it's smart for us to be seen together?" He did not say anything in reply—there wasn't anything to say, really—and she went on, pressing her point, chiding him in no uncertain terms, "*You* shouldn't have called *me*. That was dumb. And you shouldn't have gone by Morgan's house. That was even dumber. It was stupid. I said I would be in touch as soon as I could. You should have waited."

Rick knew he should have waited to hear from her—that was the plan they had agreed to beforehand, the smart way—but he hadn't counted on the vacuumlike pressure of feeling abandoned, without any communication whatsoever. He hadn't counted on the doubts he would have. He started to say something to that effect, but Karen had already moved on, giving him no chance, breathlessly recounting events.

Rick looked up and looked out the window.

The call had been so unexpected, it had thrown him, and after he hung up with Karen, Rick left his apartment, leaving even before he decided where to go. It was his day off, both at the department and at the moving company, and for a while he just drove around before he decided to have lunch.

He stopped at a local seafood restaurant, sat as far away as he could from the noisy TV, ordered a beer and a shot of Jack Daniel's. As an afterthought, he ordered the soft-shelled crab special. When the drinks came, he drank most of the shot down fast and sipped on the beer, absently watching the noontime news but still, in his head, hearing Karen, hearing her voice.

He held the table knife in both hands and flexed it, feeling the tension in the rounded, dull blade.

She had seen him parked across the street, Karen had said, when she had driven off with Stan Lee. Before the fire. She had seen just the front of his car. It had made her feel kind of tingly, seeing him there in the alley, waiting. It had made the hair rise up on the back of her neck.

Rick put the knife down, finished his beer, signaled the waitress to bring him another.

The race across the Causeway had worked perfectly. She had beaten Stan Lee easily, just as she had known that she would, and after that Stan Lee hadn't even wanted to go back to his shop—that was a break. She had dropped him off at a diner, three blocks away. *She* hadn't seen anyone else in the warehouse. Had he?

"Yes," Rick said when the waitress came over to ask him if he wanted another shot, too.

Not that it mattered now, anyway, because the police were convinced that Stan Lee had set fire to his own building, just like she had predicted. Stan Lee was a moron. Who *wouldn't* think he had done it?

"Not that it mattered," Rick repeated to himself, beginning to feel the effect of the liquor.

At any rate, the up-side was, she had his money, cash, just like he had asked for, nothing bigger than a fifty, mostly twenties and tens, and besides that, she really would like to see him. Doing *that* by yourself got old pretty fast. He had spoiled her. So how did he think they should go about it? It had to be someplace where no one would see them, of course . . .

"Wait," Rick said out loud, mimicking Karen's voice, chuckling to himself at how well she had played it. "I have an idea."

Rick finished the shot of Jack Daniel's and smacked the small, heavy glass on the table.

"I have an idea, too," he said to Karen's voice in his head.

# 24

"Skinny can't believe it," Skinny said to Ruth, jumping back up into his truck, shaking his head. "You have to sight him against a street sign to make sure he's moving at all." He put the truck in gear and pulled away, forgetful of closing the door. "How much does it take—?" he began, but he stopped abruptly because the open, driver's-side door nicked the side of the pay phone and slammed shut with resounding force.

Skinny raised his elbow protectively and scooted toward the middle of the seat.

Ruth ducked down, as if they had been in a collision.

"Who?" she asked, once she had figured out what had happened; but by then Skinny was leaning way out the window, assessing the damage to his paint. "Who do you have to sight against a street sign?" she asked patiently, when he leaned back inside. "Theriot?" she surmised tentatively, since Skinny had been calling him with harassment-level frequency since early that morning.

"What a place to put a phone," Skinny observed, agitated by the placement of the pole.

"It's right where it was when you parked next to it," Ruth remarked.

Skinny glanced at her pointedly, his eyes narrowed.

Ruth smiled agreeably.

"You bet, Theriot," Skinny said finally, making a face. "Who else?" He checked the truck, front and back, before he started forward again, and on the second try made it without incident away from the convenience store that was not far from Morgan Barrett's house. For a good part of the afternoon and into the evening, Skinny and Ruth had been watching the house, hoping to see where Karen went.

"It took him half the day to find out that Karen paid cash for her car," Skinny went on. "That piece of work took two phone calls. Two phone calls."

"I don't exactly understand that part," Ruth interjected. "What difference does it make how Karen paid for her car?"

Skinny shifted gears once, then quickly shifted again.

"It shows she had cash," he explained. "Plenty of it. By itself, that's not conclusive, but it gives us a good reason to poke around with her cash bonus. Once we're poking, we'll see exactly what she got the bonus *for*."

"But we already know that," Ruth said. "She got the bonus for borrowing to invest."

"We *think* we know," Skinny corrected her. "We haven't seen anything on paper."

A car coming the other way blinked its lights, and Skinny turned on his headlights.

"We're going to have to follow the money to lock onto her motive," he went on. "The appraiser will help, too."

Late that afternoon, Theriot had finally found an appraiser Grover and Morgan had used. While the appraiser had said he didn't know anything about any "flips," he had remembered

Karen. He had remembered that she had said she was an *investor*.

"It's all written down somewhere," Skinny added. "There are contracts, agreements, letters back and forth—you can count on that. Unless Skinny is seriously mistaken, these people"—he waved his hand in a way that indicated the conspicuous affluence of the neighborhood they were entering—"these people don't do business on a handshake."

"Don't sound so put off by that," Ruth said, smiling, but serious, too. "All that paperwork is what gives Ruth job security."

"Some security," Skinny retorted.

"I'll have another job by next week," Ruth predicted.

"Skinny doesn't doubt that," Skinny said, meaning it—and glad that they had veered away from the topic more immediately at hand. What he did not want to get into was what in the last few hours he had only begun to suspect, that Karen and Stan Lee had struck some sort of deal. That possibility bothered him considerably. If it were true—and it was the only way he could make it all fit—it meant he had been taken in several times already. It meant that Stan Lee had very likely burned his own building and that any hostility between Stan Lee and Karen was nothing more than an act. More importantly, it meant that their motives could very easily be confused and making a case against them both would be extremely difficult, if not impossible, unless he could play them one against the other, which he doubted. That was why he was anxious to keep an eye on Morgan's house, to see whether or not Karen and Stan Lee got together. Theriot was working to get a court order for a tap on Karen's phone, but if his present pace was any indication, the next monthly bill would arrive before the tap was in place.

"Have you met Stan Lee?" Skinny asked Ruth, revealing just a piece of his thoughts.

Ruth shook her head and turned sideways on the seat, facing Skinny and casually bracing herself with one hand on the dash.

"I know who he is," she replied, "and I've seen his picture, of course."

"Right," Skinny affirmed, remembering the presentation Grover had given at the party, the way it had ended. "Stan Lee gives Skinny the creeps," Skinny said, preferring not to think about the party.

"He's kind of creepy looking," Ruth agreed, "even in pictures. There's something wrong with his eyes—that's not just the pictures, either, is it?"

"No," Skinny replied absently. Several blocks ahead, near Morgan's house, he saw headlights, and he was trying to determine the make of the car behind them. "It's not just the pictures. There's something wrong with *Stan Lee*."

"He needs a better dentist," Ruth added. "Those caps—" she began, but she didn't finish her sentence because without warning Skinny sped up rather than slowed down at a corner—and went right past a stop sign.

"That's her," he explained, his voice edged with a sudden excitement. The Ford passed, going the opposite direction; Skinny put the wheel of the truck over hard and slid right through the intersection.

"Jesus," Ruth said, unconsciously using Skinny's own favorite expression.

The truck bounced against a curb as it came out of the turn.

Ruth bounced against the inside of the door.

"That's Karen," Skinny said positively. "That's the car Morgan loans her."

Across the broad median, Ruth had not seen the car very well—she had not seen who was inside it at all—so she did not say anything to Skinny but looked straight ahead, watching the car's taillights in the distance, using her hands to search for her seat belt.

"Where's my seat belt?" she asked when she couldn't find it.

"Skinny took out the seat belts," Skinny replied. "They were always in the way."

"Terrific," Ruth remarked, and tried for a good grip on the edge of the seat.

Skinny revved the engine up high and shifted hard, driving, for Skinny, perilously fast. The truck clattered noisily and seemed, somehow, to become much lighter. Overhead, the trees' branches made it seem as if they were in a very dark tunnel that opened suddenly when the trees stopped. They lost sight of the car then saw it again when they rounded the curve in the road.

"She's headed into town," Skinny figured when he saw which way Karen turned at the highway.

"Maybe she's just going to the office," Ruth offered, trying not to look but unable to keep her eyes off the speedometer. "Maybe she just forgot her purse."

"She doesn't carry a purse," Skinny noted, and accelerated again, trying to make the light where Karen had turned.

Ruth lost her grip on the seat just in time for the sudden change in direction.

Skinny made the light, screeched onto the highway across three lanes of traffic, straightened up and accelerated again, smiling slightly, obviously impressed that he had made it.

Ruth again bounced against the inside of the door.

She started to say something but decided to hold off until just before the next turn, glad for her forbearance when Skinny suddenly slowed down on his own.

The car stayed several hundred yards ahead of them and turned onto the expressway; but as Skinny slowed further, it began to pull away.

"Why are you slowing down?" Ruth asked, trying without much success to convey some concern for the chase.

"Skinny doesn't want her to see us," Skinny replied happily. "She knows the truck—I gave her a ride to Grover's party."

Ruth accepted that, refusing to ask why, if that was the case, he had sped up after her in the first place. She relaxed her grip on the seat.

"Besides that," Skinny went on, "Skinny knows where she's going, if she *is* going to meet with Stan Lee." He saw that Ruth had taken out a cigarette and reached over and pushed in the lighter.

"How do you know where she's going?" Ruth asked, genuinely puzzled.

"Skinny put it together," Skinny replied smugly, not volunteering any further information.

Ruth saw Skinny's expression and knew it was a little too smug for him to remain silent for long; so she did not ask another question but waited him out. She rolled down the window, put her arm on the sill, and when the lighter popped, lit her cigarette, turning her head to blow the smoke out the window.

"You might not have been there," Skinny added finally, "but Skinny knows you've seen pictures."

Ruth thought about that for a moment, then said very dryly, "We're going to the Superdome?"

"Like that," Skinny replied, enjoying his momentary advantage, "but smaller and flatter."

# 25

Stan Lee heard a voice. At first, he wasn't sure whether or not he was dreaming, but then he heard it again, a woman's voice, low and uncertain, calling out softly. He heard the unmistakable crunch of a footstep on the embers downstairs.

It was pitch black in the warehouse—the power had been disconnected since the day of the fire—and Stan Lee sat up slowly, careful not to disturb the empty beer cans where he had placed them by his side. He felt around for the length of pipe he kept by the cardboard he used for a bed. He found his shoes and put them on.

Even though it was no longer his, Stan Lee had continued to camp out in the warehouse. He liked it there. He liked the quiet and the dark. It reminded him of the times he and Mitchell had camped out in his daddy's old Airstream trailer. He had thought of Mitchell a lot in the last few days; he had even thought of his daddy. It was about time for him to go on back home, he figured, once he had settled up with whoever it was had killed his partner—and he already had a pretty good idea what to do about that. He and Mitchell, they should probably never have come to the city in the first place.

Stan Lee picked up the pipe and carefully made his way to the top of the stairs. He moved slowly in the darkness, feeling his way along, listening for the sound of the voice. It was probably a couple of teenagers, he figured, looking for a place for humpin', and if he worked it right, he might get a good peek at the action before he put the fear of God into them for sneaking in and disturbing his sleep.

There.

There was the voice again. A low call—and this time there was a reply.

Stan Lee found the stairs and went down them, moving cautiously, one step at a time. He saw the beam from a flashlight and heard the low murmuring of conversation. He wasn't twenty feet away when he heard a shout. Immediately thereafter, the first gunshot exploded. He saw a flash of yellow light and felt the concussing force of the shot, more like a slap than a sound. He heard a grunt, a grunt and a sigh put together.

Then there was another shot.

And another.


Karen could not believe her good luck. She had seen Skinny behind her—she had noticed the truck as soon as it swung around so abruptly—and she had not known what to do. So she had simply gone on, just driving a little faster than usual, and she had lost him. He had missed the entrance to the expressway, she supposed, and was doubling back, trying to catch her.

*No way*, she thought, *not even in this car*, and she kept the accelerator on the floor all the way to downtown, to the exit that put her out closest to the burned-out warehouse. She went around the block once before she parked on the next street, got out of the car and walked up the alley, glad that she had thought to bring along a flashlight. She could feel the sweat on her palms on the revolver's black rubber grips. She could feel her heart in her chest. She knew better than to stop, not even for a second. Not when she saw Rick's car, parked in close to the dumpster. Not when she saw the side door to the shop, already forced open. She slipped through the door, turned on the flashlight, and played it over the fire-blackened office. She saw the metal desk, warped by heat and already rusting, an overturned chair, the scorched remains of a calendar on the far wall. When she had fixed her way to the inner door, she turned off the flashlight long enough to go through it and went out into the shop.

"Rick?" she called tentatively, her voice low.

Her foot crunched an ember.

"Rick?" she called again.

"I am too going in," Ruth said adamantly. "I'm not about to sit out here by myself, not in this neighborhood."

"There's nobody around here at night," Skinny argued.

"I *know* there's nobody around here at night, which is why I'm going with you."

"Jesus Christ on a platter," Skinny said, exasperated to the point of concession.

Skinny had pulled up by the front corner of the warehouse just a few moments before, right after Karen had made her tour of the block and gone in through the alley; and he had asked Ruth to wait in the truck. Her response, he had to admit, was not totally unexpected.

"Okay," he conceded, not wanting to waste any more time, "but you stay behind Skinny. And you do what he says."

"Ruth will stay behind Skinny," Ruth half-agreed, and opened the door on her side of the truck.

"Leave the door open," Skinny ordered.

Ruth got out and pushed the door closed until it shut quietly, with a click.

Skinny pretended not to notice but patted his back near his kidney, checking the position of his pistol. He glanced at Ruth and went on down the alley, stepping out with his overlong strides, flapping his arms, not looking back. At the side door to the shop, he checked to be sure she was with him then went inside, moving forward slowly, feeling for Ruth. In the darkness, he felt her belt and looped two fingers through it; with his other hand, he took out the Colt and quietly thumbed off the safety. He could hear voices, a man's and a woman's, but he could not make out the words. He kept moving forward, sidestepping, pulling Ruth along until he bumped into the edge of the door.

"I would have done anything for you," the man said, his voice low and intense. "Don't you know that?"

As soon as Skinny heard the voice, he knew two things at once: whoever was speaking was not Stan Lee, and whoever it was had been drinking heavily. The liquor was there in the tone, in the slur to the words and in the overstressed enunciation. Skinny moved forward again, enough to look out into the shop.

"But it was always the package, wasn't it? Your package. Putting it together."

"I have to have it," Karen affirmed coolly. "I have to."

Karen was only about fifteen feet away, holding her flashlight aimed down, at an angle. The man was beyond the pool of light the flashlight cast on the floor, nothing more than a shape in the darkness, a shape and a voice.

"I should have known," the man went on. "That's what I tell myself, that I should have known. But known what, Karen?" The shape lurched forward, then steadied itself. "You made it sound so simple. I burn down the building, and you pay me enough to cover my bills. You complete your package and there we are, happy ever after."

Skinny could not believe his ears—and *his* good luck. He had convinced himself that Stan Lee had set fire to his own shop and because of that had assumed that Karen was meeting Stan Lee there in the warehouse, where likely he was still living; and while he had been completely wrong, the faulty reasoning had nevertheless brought him right to the arsonist.

"Happy ever after," the man repeated, his tone mocking, and mean.

Suddenly, Skinny felt Ruth's presence, and he realized that she had come up beside him. He started to push her back, to give himself room to move if he had to, but he saw the man lurch forward again. At the same time, Karen raised the flashlight, and he saw the gun in the man's hand.

"You're the only one who can connect me to this," he said, waving the pistol in a way that indicated the warehouse. "At least I'll be back at zero."

"Freeze, son of a bitch," Skinny shouted, and wheeled through the door, bringing his own pistol up, holding it in both hands, away from his body. His shoulder bumped Ruth, hard, and knocked her back, out of the way.

A gunshot exploded, and for a fraction of a second Skinny

thought *he* had fired because he had been watching the man's pistol and had not seen a flash from the muzzle.

The man sagged.

A second shot followed the first.

Skinny wheeled again then wheeled back quickly at the sound of another shot, in time to see the man's pistol discharge without effect as he slumped to the floor. Out of the corner of his eye, Skinny saw the glint of light on a long silver revolver, *his* revolver, but before he could turn he heard the distinctive thud-smack of steel against flesh; and the flashlight suddenly went out.

"Shit," he swore, not moving, unable to see.

In the darkness, he heard a man groan.

"I have a lighter," Ruth volunteered.

Skinny reached toward her voice, found her hand and took the lighter, flicking it on as soon as he had turned it around. He went through the door and out into the shop, holding the flickering flame up high, trying to get the most from the dim light it cast.

The man was just where he had been, on the floor. His chest was covered with blood. Briefly, Skinny swung the light away, facing back to where Karen had been. He saw his silver gun and nearby what looked like blood on the side of a column. He turned back, considering the distance, and saw a length of pipe on the floor.

"Jesus Christ," he said, feeling a chill run right up his spine, knowing immediately what had happened. "Where's Karen?"

# 26

Stan Lee had moved very quickly. The shout had startled him but for some reason the first shot had put him in motion—likely it was all the practice he had had ducking bullets and ricochets the times Mitchell had had too much to drink and had taken to firing his pistol rapid-fire. He had moved straight toward the sound of the shot, seen who had fired, and when Karen fired again, he had swung his pipe hard, catching her right across the ear, dropping her like a sack of potatoes. She had bounced against a column on her way down, and he had grabbed her and grabbed the flashlight, too, all in one motion. He had turned the flashlight off, left his pipe, and run back the length of the shop, Karen over his shoulder, easily finding his way out, even in darkness. He hoped to hell he hadn't killed her—he had plans for this little bitch.

At his car, he fished in his pocket for his keys, opened the trunk, and unceremoniously dropped Karen in.

She hit the floor of the trunk with a thud.

Stan Lee could not see if she was breathing, so he reached between her legs, found a good, fleshy area, and gave her a brutally hard pinch, twisting the skin as he did so, smiling broadly at the sound of her moan.

He shut the trunk and scurried around to the side of his car.

Skinny had heard the door open. Just after he had seen Stan Lee's piece of pipe on the floor—the same one, he suspected, that Stan Lee had used on him, pressing the end of it behind his ear to make him think it was the barrel of a shotgun—he had heard a sound that hadn't really registered until he had realized Stan Lee had been in the shop. He had heard the door near the front of the warehouse, the small one on the side opposite the office. He had heard a faint creak when it opened.

"Can you take care of him?" Skinny asked Ruth, indicating the man on the floor, knowing there was not much she could do to help him. "Skinny's going to get help," he added, before she could reply.

Ruth had moved near the man and was kneeling down beside him. She nodded, her eyes fixed on the man's blood-covered chest. Even in the dim light from the lighter, her face appeared pale and drawn.

Skinny quickly retrieved his silver gun and moved beside her. He checked for a path to the office door, then gave Ruth the lighter, pressing it into her hand after he had allowed the flame to go out. In the darkness, he placed his hand over hers and gave it a squeeze. As soon as he took his hand away, Ruth flicked on the lighter.

"Be careful," she said, but Skinny was already gone.

*　　　*　　　*

Even though it was dark outside, it wasn't as dark as it had been in the warehouse, and Skinny moved at high speed, doubling the pace of his overlong strides, double-timing his flapping arms, going down the alley, away from his truck, trying to remember exactly the map Ruth had shown him of the area. There were two alleys, he knew, and if he remembered correctly, a way to get from one to the other, a very narrow space between the backs of the buildings. He had not seen Stan Lee's canary-yellow car when he pulled up in front of the warehouse, and he felt fairly certain that, if Stan Lee had not parked in one alley, he had parked in the other. He nearly went past the narrow space before he saw it, a shoulder-wide opening as dark as it had been in the warehouse. He held his forearms in front of his face and went through it as fast as he could, feeling his way along with his elbows, stepping high, trying not to kick the assorted debris on the ground. He saw light at the end of the space, a dim slice of it framed by the parallel corners of the buildings, at the same time that he heard a car's trunk lid slammed shut. He heard a car door opened and closed. Before he went out into the alley, he stopped to look: not ten feet away, to his left, was Stan Lee's car, with Stan Lee in it, behind the wheel, fitting the key into the ignition.

"No shit," he said to himself, and shifted his silver gun to his right hand. He slid down beside the car and, reaching through the still-broken driver's-side window, jammed the barrel of the revolver right behind Stan Lee's left ear. "Freeze right there, peckerwood," he said to Stan Lee, pleased that he had thought to say it. "This isn't a piece of three-quarter-inch pipe," he added, just to make things perfectly clear.

Stan Lee froze, but only for a second.

"It's the skinny man," he said, his tone half amused. "The one looks like a scarecrow."

He turned the ignition key on, and the car started.

With his left hand, Skinny reached into the car and grabbed Stan Lee's ear.

"Skinny's got you, Stan Lee," Skinny explained, exerting pressure, pulling with his left hand and pushing with his right, trying to twist Stan Lee around but feeling his grip start to slip.

"You won't shoot me," Stan Lee predicted, apparently numb to his ear. "I ain't done nothing wrong." Calmly, he put the car in reverse and started to roll backward.

Skinny did lose his grip then, and momentarily he looked down, at his hand, wondering what had made Stan Lee's ear so slippery. He wiped his hand on the thigh of his jeans.

"Wait a minute," he said, looking back up. "Wait a minute, Stan Lee." He waved his hand in a conciliatory way. "Before you go, Skinny's got a question."

Stan Lee obligingly stopped the car and put it out of gear. He smoothed back his hair and rested one arm on the sill.

"What's that?" he asked, smiling confidently, showing just the tips of the caps on his teeth.

"Stan Lee," Skinny said, moving up to Stan Lee's window, "Skinny meant to ask, did you remember to post the reward?"

Stan Lee's smile broadened, and he ducked his head, up and down.

"I sure did," he replied. "I took the money in yesterday. Cash. You should'a seen their faces."

"Hot damn," Skinny said, and he leaned on Stan Lee's arm, pinning it down on the sill, and unhesitatingly he smacked him on the side of the head with the side of his silver revolver, knowing when Stan Lee went out like a light why he liked his silver gun best.

"Hot damn," he said again, pushed Stan Lee over, and got into the car.

# 27

Bayou Barataria is a very heavily trafficked inland waterway that runs from the town of Lafitte, named after the famous pirate, of course, all the way to Grand Isle, a large island close-in on the Gulf of Mexico. The bayou is lined on both sides with houses built to accommodate a boat first, then people, and with various facilities and companies that serve the offshore oil industry. Huge barges pushed by tugs, steel crew boats, shrimp boats with nets hanging, private fishing boats of every description all ply the gray-brown water, making their way to the gulf or back, going after or carrying brown shrimp or redfish, king mackerel, pompano, or oil.

Out on the bayou, Skinny's boat, the *No Special Hurry*, seemed to lift and to smooth out as it got up to speed. Perched on its stern, spray flying behind it, it left a wake that rocked the boats moored on both sides of the bayou. Perched on the elevated captain's chair anchored near the stern, one hand on the steering wheel that moved the powerful outboard motor, Skinny steered, dodging in and out among the various vessels that got in his way, almost every one of them substantially larger than his twenty-foot boat. Sitting backward on the front seat, her knees as high as her chest and her arms wrapped around them, was Ruth; between Skinny and Ruth was Mike Theriot, still wearing the tie he had worn from the office. The sun was high overhead, too high, really, to be setting out, but even Skinny hadn't complained more than a little when their earlier activities had taken longer than expected.

Skinny and Mike Theriot had agreed that the reward money should be shared with Ruth, and that morning the three of them had gone to claim it, a profitable morning by any standard since each of them had come away with a check for over thirteen thousand dollars. Despite his severe wounds, Rick Trask had recovered and had testified against Karen. While out on appeal of her reduced-charge conviction, Karen had officially completed her package and signed up the tenants for her new development, which would, for five years, undoubtedly make her the richest woman in St. Gabriel's Women's Prison. The various charges against Stan Lee had been dropped when he had promised to go on back home and never come back. Grover and Morgan, it was rumored, were under some scrutiny by various governmental agencies, including the IRS. Skinny had been reinstated on the condition that he let Mike Theriot drive most of the time. Ruth had found a new job at a bank.

Mike Theriot reached into the red Igloo cooler and took out a beer which he offered to Skinny, who refused, and to Ruth, who accepted.

"What are you going to do with the money?" Mike Theriot asked Ruth, taking out another beer for himself, speaking loudly enough for his voice to carry over the sound of the motor.

"I don't know," Ruth replied, smiling as she popped open the can and took her first sip. "Put it in the bank, I guess. Worry about how to hold onto it."

The looming side of a barge suddenly appeared, the heavy steel plates close enough to touch. Mike Theriot turned to look back as the barge slipped behind them, then his gaze shifted from the barge to Skinny, his expression showing his concerned disapproval.

"What are you going to do?" Ruth asked when he turned back.

Mike Theriot shook his head in a way that conveyed two things: the uncertain future of his share of the money and his doubt that, with Skinny driving, he'd ever get to spend it.

"What I'd like to do *first*," he said, glancing back again to underscore his point, "I'd like to go to a market and *buy* us some fish."

"*Buy* fish?" Skinny asked, his normal speaking voice easily heard. He shook his head side to side. "Jesus Christ."

"It's too late now, anyway," Ruth observed to Mike Theriot. "We're already here."

"We're already here," Mike Theriot repeated, feigning a gloomy discomfort he dispelled with a quick smile he made sure Skinny couldn't see.

Ruth laughed at Mike Theriot's smile, then her expression fell into a good-humored grin as she looked around, enjoying the day. On shore, she saw a brown pelican standing on a stump, making a show of folding its large wings. The odd, prehistoric-looking bird watched them curiously, turning its head to see them with one eye, then the other, obviously unable to figure out what to make of them. Ruth glanced from the pelican to Skinny, amused when she saw all the features they had in common—alarmed when she realized

Skinny had seen the pelican, too, and was turning back toward it as with his left hand he reached for his silver revolver in the holster attached to his seat.

"Don't shoot it," she said, but her words were lost in the changing, whining pitch of the motor.

The small boat slid, seeming to pivot as much as to turn. Water came in over the gunwales.

"Don't shoot it," she said again, but Skinny fired.

The bullet hit to the left of the pelican, splattering mud on the bank.

The boat straightened out, on a collision course with the stump.

Skinny fired again and quickly cut the throttle.

The pelican flew off, shrieking.

The boat rocked forward, caught in the surge of water it had made in the turn, and before the surge passed and went on to shore, leaving it rocking gently, almost motionless, Ruth saw a pair of eyes just above the surface of the water and the long, ominous shape of the body behind them.

The alligator sank straight down in the water.

"Did you hit it?" Mike Theriot asked, looking over the side of the boat.

Skinny shook his head, and put the silver revolver back in the holster. "Skinny wasn't trying to hit anything," he explained. "Skinny was just making noise." He looked at Ruth and smiled brightly. "But he sure had Ruth fooled."

Ruth watched the pelican as it leveled off, moving away, not quite so clumsy in flight. When the bird had disappeared from view, she looked back at Skinny.

"Skinny doesn't fool Ruth," Ruth replied. "Not for a second."